"I was an interesting child, to say the least." Zed chuckled.

"You obviously haven't changed."

He gazed at her. "Should I take that as a compliment?"

"Most definitely."

He warmed at her kind words, and an idea came to him. "Tasha, question for you. Do your friends give you a hard time about not being married?"

"Uh, yeah. All the time."

"Mine, too. Ad nauseam." He whooshed out a long breath. "What if I told you I may have a way for you to make some substantial cash to achieve your business dream, as well as get your friends off your back about marriage once and for all?"

A flicker of concern flashed across her face, and he sensed her guard was going up. He got it. He was virtually a stranger and she didn't know where he was going with the conversation.

Zed gulped, as if readying himself to be submerged under water for a lengthy period, then uttered words he never thought he'd say. "I was thinking we could get married."

C.J. Carroll loves movies, history, literature and the arts. She is a hopeless romantic who first started telling stories as a child with her sixty-plus Barbie and Ken doll collection. C.J. loves chick lit and believes chocolate should top the food pyramid. Additionally, C.J. is a huge aerospace and NASA fan. She hopes that her stories entertain and uplift, and that her readers feel the loving touch of God's hand. C.J. resides in Denver, Colorado, with her cat, Monkey.

Books by C.J. Carroll

Love Inspired

Claiming His Christmas Inheritance

Visit the Author Profile page at Harlequin.com.

Claiming His Christmas Inheritance

C.J. Carroll

LOVE INSPIRED
INSPIRATIONAL ROMANCE

LOVE INSPIRED®
INSPIRATIONAL ROMANCE

Recycling programs
for this product may
not exist in your area.

ISBN-13: 978-1-335-56735-2

Claiming His Christmas Inheritance

Copyright © 2021 by Cheryl Elizabeth Jackson

This edition published by arrangement with Harlequin Books S.A.

For questions and comments about the quality of this book, please contact us
at CustomerService@Harlequin.com.

Love Inspired
22 Adelaide St. West, 40th Floor
Toronto, Ontario M5H 4E3, Canada
www.Harlequin.com

Printed in U.S.A.

And the Lord answered me, and said,
Write the vision, and make it plain upon tables,
that he may run that readeth it.
—*Habakkuk* 2:2

This book is dedicated to my mom, M.J. Carroll, who always believed in my dream to become an author and who is now my guardian angel.

Acknowledgments

I'd like to thank "my girls," who always believed and supported my writing dream: Tamera Trueblood, Dina Kauffman, Cantel Brown, Maryann San Antonio, Latrievette Garcia, Anjali Baughman, Cassandra France, Diane Nelson, Sydney White, Diane Thornton, Kim Church, Tamara Conley, Judy Sherman, Helen Gray, Alex Robinson, Carmine Lapsley Haynes, Katie Ford, Vicky Hildner, Claire Brownell, Nancy Nicely, Bonnie Hahn, Allison Riola, Haley Osborn, Freddie Davis, Cindy Fane, Bridget Arend, Ginger Maloney, Mary Marcus, Michele Towers, Jendayi Harris, Shelly Urban, Kathy Keairns, Kathy Matzen, Beverly Jones, Karen Drew, Bettina Klattfaistnauer and Jodi James.

Also, thanks to Carolyn and Isaiah Roach, Leta and Steve Strom, Gina and Don Burman, Pam and John McDermott, Ray and Lonna Whitaker.

And thank you Antonio McGee (my best guy friend), Taylor Ohlsen, John McCloud (and Ansley), Jim Williams, Ron Olin, Chris Fry, Tom Radigan and my CU/DU crew!

Finally, I'd like to thank my editor, Dina Davis, who has an amazing editor's eye, has been wonderfully supportive and took a chance on me.

Chapter One

Tasha Jenkins's heart fluttered wildly, like the tiny wings of a baby bird. She squeezed her eyelids shut. "You can do it, girl. You got this."

It's my first Christmas alone in the world.

Her eyes flickered open, and she stared at the familiar purple Victorian in front of her. A salmon-stained sky, dotted with wispy, cottonball clouds, provided a splendid backdrop to the spectacular structure.

Every Christmas since Tasha was eight, she and her single mother had visited the historic Avenue Parkway neighborhood of Vista Peak, Colorado. They loved to admire the turn-of-the-twentieth-century homes' holiday decorations.

Although it wasn't the fanciest or most ornately decorated house in the neighborhood, the purple Victorian was their favorite. Its charming amenities, unusual color and the sense of home and family it evoked for them contributed to the special feeling they both had about the place.

But this time there was an empty spot beside her where her mom used to stand, clasping her hand.

Tasha admired the house's wraparound porch, decorative turret and scalloped shingles. Her gaze roamed lovingly over the carved columns, spindles, ornate molding and lavender trim. Three massive evergreens, lightly dusted with snow, surrounded the house like stoic sentinels.

A large white wreath hung on the front door. Multicolored ornaments filled several oversize vintage lanterns on the porch. Giant red-and-green peppermints on sticks, a nativity scene and a miniature Christmas village were displayed in the yard.

She bit her lip and peered heavenward. *Lord, I miss my mom. She was my North Star.* Sorrow at the unfairness of her mother's untimely death, after a hard life, threatened to consume her. *Can You hear me, Lord? Do You really care?* Grief shredded her heart.

A vehicle door abruptly slammed behind her, and Tasha turned to discover a tall, brown-skinned man exiting a silver Ford F-150 truck.

She quickly wiped away rogue tears.

"Miss, are you okay?" The inherent kindness gleaming from his eyes nearly did her in.

"Yeah. I will be," she said.

Narrowly built, but muscular and defined, the man appeared well over six feet tall. While his crisp white shirt, a forest green-and-red plaid sweater-vest, gold bow tie, black pants and vintage wingtip shoes he wore harkened to another era, the stranger appeared to be around her age—in his mid to late thirties.

"Quite a beauty," he said.

Shocked at his full-frontal approach, Tasha blushed at the compliment. She was grateful her cinnamon-brown skin hid physical signs of embarrassment—especially when she realized he was looking past her.

Oh my, he meant the house, not me.

Tasha quickly recovered. "That it is," she replied as if she understood his intent all along.

He scrutinized her. Understanding lit his features, and he grinned. "You thought I was complimenting you."

She winced. She'd never mastered keeping a neutral face. "Guilty as charged."

A deep-throated, hardy chuckle escaped his lips. Irises the color of sunlight shimmering through honey observed her. "Wait one moment while I uninsert my foot from my mouth."

She raised her hand in protest. "No worries."

"You know, the compliment most definitely

works both ways." His eyes grazed her face like a gentle breeze caressing a flower.

Tasha willed her heart to continue to beat normally. *Oh, the brotha's got game. Slow your roll, playa-playa. Your charm won't work on me. Even if you are as fine as Mr. Michael B. Jordan, Mr. Bradley Cooper and Mr. Idris Elba combined. With a cherry on top.*

Nevertheless, she had to acknowledge his kudos was nice. "Thank you," she replied.

Embarrassed and eager to move on, Tasha earnestly returned her attention to the grand edifice in front of them. She hugged herself against the brisk air. "Visiting this house has been a Christmas tradition for me since childhood. I used to come here with my mom, Violet-Sage. She died in January. This is my first Christmas without her." Her throat tightened.

The stranger's expression radiated compassion. "I'm sorry for your loss." His deep voice, tenderized by sympathy, touched her.

"Thank you. Coming here for the first time without her is hard. Visiting this Victorian and Union Station in Denver afterward was our annual Christmas holiday ritual. That's where I'm headed next."   .

His happy countenance dissolved at the mention of Union Station. Why? Most people loved the iconic, historic place.

Emotions swirled within her at the thought of her new normal without her mother, and fresh tears filled her eyes.

The man produced a crisp white handkerchief from his pocket. She couldn't hide her surprise at his outdated gesture. She'd only seen men use handkerchiefs in old movies.

He grinned. Killer dimples appeared, more potent than kryptonite. "I'm kinda old-school." He handed her the handkerchief.

Tasha took the hankie and dabbed her eyes. The crisply folded cotton material smelled faintly of his woodsy cologne, and she resisted the urge to deeply inhale the wonderful scent.

She returned it to him. "Thank you."

He placed the handkerchief in his pocket. "The holidays must be hard without your mom."

"My only consolation is that she is in no pain now and that she's with God, and one day I'll see her again. She was my true north, my only family." Tasha heard the warble in her voice.

"I get it." His countenance darkened. "Both my parents are gone, too."

She sensed further subtext in his statement, but he didn't elaborate.

Tasha tried to collect herself. "My dad was never in the picture. I think my mom's secret fantasy was to meet someone someday, fall hopelessly in love and live in a grand house like this one."

The man studied the Victorian before gazing up at the patches of blue sky, which peeked between the pink clouds. His view finally settled back on her. "Maybe your mom's looking down from heaven, praying the same thing for you one day."

Tasha half chuckled, half snorted. Mortification engulfed her. Her awkward, quirky cackle was not pleasant. "Uh, yeah—no. She'd know that would be a waste of time." She'd had her heart sliced, diced and served back to her cold one too many times by men to care anymore. Rejection had shattered her hopes.

The guy's eyebrows leaped in apparent surprise.

Chin defiantly elevated, she met his gaze. "Marriage is not the endgame for every woman," she sternly declared.

He raised his hands in surrender, regret rolling across his face. "Sorry. My bad. I shouldn't have presumed."

Her heart melted. She hadn't meant to sound so testy. "It's okay. I should be used to such assumptions by now. The idea about my mom watching over me was a nice thought, though." She produced a smile, hoping it softened her blunt words.

Down the street a large truck with a tractor

bed chugged toward them. It roared past, rumbling like an angry mechanical beast. The massive vehicle left a charcoal-black cloud of smoke as a parting gift.

Tasha guessed the big rig was probably headed somewhere in the neighborhood, carrying cargo to build yet another modern plywood-boxed Mc-Mansion—functional, yet devoid of character. Sadly, even small towns like Vista Peak weren't immune to the rapidly changing landscape of neighborhoods that bigger cities like Denver were facing.

They covered their mouths against the noxious fumes, until the haze dissipated.

The stranger held out his hand. "I'm Zedrick, by the way. My friends call me Zed."

Tasha shook his hand. She liked the way his big, sturdy hand, corded with robust veins, swallowed her slender fingers in a secure grip.

She noticed he didn't offer a last name. Maybe his off-the-chart good looks made him an easy target for lady social media trackers.

If her assumption was correct, he needn't have worried. She considered love a four-letter word. Tasha knew people found this a bit ironic, considering her profession as a wedding planner.

Truth be told, she was a hopeless romantic— when it came to other people. *I'm the vaccine to love. I'm immune, playa.*

"I'm Tasha," she replied. *Two can play at your no-last-name game.* She returned her gaze to the house, before observing him again. "Are you a fan of the place, too?"

An odd look flashed across his face. It quickly disappeared. His jaw flexed. "You could say that."

Zed's phone chimed, and he removed it from his pants pocket and peered at the screen. A look of regret crossed his face. "Sorry. I should take this call."

"No worries," she said. "I should probably get going. Nice meeting you."

"You, too," he replied.

Tasha headed toward her royal blue Mini Cooper parked across the street. Climbing into the vehicle, she watched Zed as he stood in front of the Victorian. He was certainly a fine-looking man with his high forehead, sharp-edged square fade haircut and chiseled features highlighted by a wide, flat nose.

However, she noticed the once-light expression on his face had turned serious. The call had obviously sobered him.

Even though he was a stranger, the call and the break in their meeting had disappointed her, and she couldn't quite figure out why.

She finally fired up the car's engine, eager to fulfill her second holiday tradition for the day, as well as celebrate her birthday. After doing a U-turn, she zipped through Vista Peak's downtown square and headed to the highway toward Denver.

When she arrived in downtown Denver and pulled into a parking place, her phone pinged. She looked at the number. Tasha rolled her eyes in exasperation. Another bill collector hot on her trail. "You can't draw blood from a turnip," she yelled at the ringing device. Frustration and weariness rolled through her.

You're not gonna bother me today. It's my birthday and I won't let you ruin it. I'm taking a vacay from all my cares and worries. She hurled the phone back in her purse.

Tasha exited her vehicle and fed the meter. She took a few deep breaths to calm her nerves and headed down the block to Union Station.

Upon approaching the building, Tasha stopped in her tracks, captivated by its majestic beauty. The stately structure stood like a proud grand dame at the edge of Denver's glittering skyscrapers. The building's Italianate design made of rhyolite, pink lava stone and limestone was even more glorious during the Christmas season because it was festooned with decorations. She lovingly observed one of her favorite features, the building's tall, narrow windows, framed by arches bearing carved columbines—Colorado's state flower.

Tasha entered the building. The loveliness of the train station's interior always left her breathless. She admired the ornately carved cream-colored crown molding and breathtaking, sparkling chandeliers.

A large Christmas tree with festive oversize ornaments towered over the east entrance. A line of people stood waiting to take selfies by the tree. Most appeared to be families. They laughed and posed, their eyes glistening with apparent love and holiday cheer.

Loneliness washed over Tasha.

Her neck tensed. Tasha soothed the muscle kink with her fingers. The worrisome bill collector had stressed her, making her long even more to be a part of the festive, carefree holiday celebrations she was witnessing. She'd once dreamed of having a family and reveling in holiday cheer, too. But that dream was dead.

The gloomy clouds in Zed's brain, temporarily held at bay by the happy diversion of meeting Tasha, regrouped and settled.

He'd wasted no words with his lawyer, Michael Shanahan, whose call had ended his conversation with Tasha. "Tell me you've got good news."

A long sigh sounded on the other end. "Sorry,

buddy. The will is iron-tight. There's no way around it."

Zed groaned. "Seriously, dude. This is ludicrous. It's as if I'm in some bad made-for-TV movie. This is unreal."

"I beg to differ, man. It's very real. Your late aunt's stipulation is that you can't have the house unless you're married for at least three months and live in the Victorian with your wife during that time. If you choose not to do so, the home is to be sold to developers to tear down and rebuild as they see fit. She was very specific about that, too."

Zed gazed at the purple Victorian standing in front of him—his childhood family home. Dual love and irritation at his aunt assaulted him.

Upon his parents' untimely deaths, when he was nineteen, Zora, who'd become a second mom to him, had obtained full ownership of the home. Because she lived out of state, she'd rented it out and deemed him a makeshift property manager of the place.

When his aunt died, he'd fully expected his beloved childhood home to become his, free and clear. It had been vacant of tenants for a few months.

"Aunt Zora," he whispered, shaking his head. Even in death, she hadn't given up on her dream to marry him off. While her over-the-top actions might seem irrational to anyone looking in from the outside, it was totally her MO. His aunt never did anything halfway. She'd obviously wanted him to know how serious she was about forcing him to at least give marriage a try. And she knew the only way she could force his hand was by making the stakes extremely high.

The will laid out a deadline for him to get married, which made sense. She knew his tendency to drag his feet. He now had less than two weeks to find a bride, because he'd dillydallied.

"Zed, are you still there?" Michael asked.

Zed shook free from his reverie. "Sorry, man. Yeah, I'm here. Thanks for trying to find an out. Catch you later." Zed ended the call.

His gaze roamed over the house. He'd felt obligated to continue to decorate the house for Christmas even though he hadn't lived in the place for years. Many people, like Tasha, stopped by annually to admire the place during the holidays.

How would Tasha have reacted if she'd known the Victorian was his childhood home? It didn't surprise him that he'd never seen her all the years she and her mom observed the house. Their family had become used to holiday clusters of people admiring the home, until their presence was almost like white noise. And most Christmases, while his dad often worked, he and his mom usually went out of town to visit his aunt.

He wanted to save the house for himself *and* those strangers like Tasha who gazed at it with dreams in their eyes. Where in the world was he going to find a woman willing to marry a stranger, and like a revolving door, just as quickly become a divorcée? Someone with similar morals and character that he could trust being in close proximity with for three months.

He also needed a lady he could easily cut ties with when the agreement was over, without messy emotions getting in the way. He'd been down that road before, where women claimed they were happy just being friends, but ultimately wanted more from him, convinced they could change his mind.

Tasha invaded his thoughts again. His heart went out to her, especially during the holidays. He knew what it was like to be alone in the world. His aunt Zora had been his last living close relative. It had given him pleasure to know that the Victorian brought Tasha joy, that something he was connected to had brightened her spirits and made her happy.

There was something as fragile as china about the diminutive stranger with the high-lighted brown shoulder-length corkscrew curls and cocoa-colored satin-smooth skin. Her features were topped off by a beautiful, Cheshire cat–like endearing smile.

If the eyes were the windows to the soul, he'd seen a latent sadness beyond the bright, inquisitive sparkle in Tasha's almond-brown eyes. Something he recognized because he'd often seen the same look in his beloved mother's eyes. The source of his mother's perpetual wounded-dove expression had been his father. The man who sacrificed his son and wife on the altar of ambition. His workaholic father's career had been his first love. His family had come in a distant second. Bile gurgled and burned Zed's throat at the thought.

He could admit that he had his father's same workaholic tendencies. But that was where the similarities ended. He'd vowed long ago to never do what his father did to his mother. His work was his first love, too. And that was the way he liked it. He wouldn't put a woman and family in second place, like his father did with his mother, leaving her with a shattered heart.

Which is why he could never marry for real.

Tasha seemed to tick both boxes he wanted for his temporary wife, with her vehement declaration that marriage wasn't every woman's endgame and the mention of her faith, which meant they had similar beliefs and she probably could be trusted. Neither of them was interested in long-term commitment. And while her emotional investment in the home was nowhere near his, she did have a special attachment to the place, so she might be more willing to help save it.

Might their meeting have been serendipitous? There was only one way to find out. Maybe he could find her at Union Station.

He quickly made his way into the house, intent on fulfilling his reason for coming there—to turn on the faucets to drip because of the subzero temperatures forecast for the night. Old houses and burst pipes were no fun. He'd been there, done that.

Afterward, he jumped in his truck and guided the vehicle toward the highway to Denver and Union Station.

As Zed's truck navigated the winding highway to the city, tension built in his gut, like a tightening fist. By the time he maneuvered his vehicle into a metered space downtown, he had to take deep breaths.

He peered at Union Station, the historic structure that he'd known so well as a child. The place mostly held sad memories of saying goodbye to his dad, a railroad executive and later an airline executive, who was often away from home, even during the holidays.

His parents had married and had him late in life. He remembered his father, his black hair speckled with gray, always distinguishably dressed, standing stoically in Union Station, as Zed cried his heart out each holiday they parted. The cavernous building would carry the sound of his cries. His dad, embarrassed at his son's public outburst, would say in an even tone, "Son, you must learn how to be a man, in control of yourself and your circumstances."

Zed had wanted to yell, *But I'm not a man. I'm a boy who wants his father home for the holidays. That's all!*

The memories had choked out any joy he had of the beautiful venue during the holidays. Until he just quit going to the place.

"You got this," he whispered to himself.

He exited the truck and headed toward the building. Streams of holiday revelers were clumped together, entering as he did. Glittering decorations adorned most surfaces, and the low buzz of excited voices filled the spacious room.

Walking just beyond the gold-roped stations that parceled off the massive Christmas tree loaded with oversize ornaments, he scanned the room, looking for Tasha's bright teal coat. When he finally caught sight of her, she was looking his way, surprise on her face. Tasha weaved through the crowd toward him.

"Are you following me?" she asked.

He was grateful to note a hint of teasing in her

voice. He certainly didn't want to come off the wrong way. "Maybe, Tasha-without-a-last-name-because-we-have-to-be-careful-these-days-and-you-don't-know-me-like-that."

Tasha's unusual cackle filled the air. "Thank you for just making my birthday." Regret instantly skewed her features. He guessed she hadn't meant to disclose this fact.

He couldn't hide his surprise. "It's your birthday?"

She grimaced. "I didn't mean to say that. I don't usually go around advertising my birthday."

"Why not? It's a big day. Everyone deserves to be celebrated on their birthday. So how was it growing up, having a birthday so near Christmas?"

She groaned. "Combined presents. Honestly, I hated it. Still going through therapy over it," she joked.

He chuckled. "Well, then, we can't let this day go by without a celebration."

She shook her head. "No, really, it's okay. I didn't tell you about it to obligate you."

"Believe me, I never do anything I don't want to do."

She observed him for a moment, as if contemplating her decision. "Okay. I'm in. And by the way, my last name is Jenkins."

"Nice to know, Ms. Jenkins. And on that note,

my last name is Evans. Do you like breakfast food?"

"Love it. I can eat breakfast any time of day."

"Great. Then how about Snooze, the breakfast place?"

"Sweet." Tasha studied him as they started to walk toward the restaurant. "Is Union Station a holiday tradition for you, too?"

He tensed up. "It used to be. I haven't been here in a long time."

"You never answered my question. Why are you here?"

"I'll explain. In time. Let's eat and celebrate you."

She wound with him through the river of people to the restaurant.

"So are you from Vista Peak?" he asked.

"No. I grew up in Denver. When I went away to college, my mom moved to Vista Peak. After college I moved there, too."

"Was that, like, a few years ago?"

"Ha. You got jokes. I'm thirty-six. It was more than a few years ago. But I liked your veiled way of finding out my age. Smooth."

He laughed. "I guess I could never be accused of being stealth. Just so you don't feel so alone in sharing, I'm thirty-eight."

While they waited to be seated, she told him a little more about herself. He was surprised to learn she was a wedding coordinator, considering her stance on marriage for herself. However, she'd admitted to being a hopeless romantic when it came to others.

"My dream is to open my own wedding-venue business to supplement the wedding planning. It would be a one-stop shop thing. Not only would couples get me as a wedding planner, but I'd provide a photographer, light catering and a simple, inexpensive quaint venue. Here's the really cool part about the business—I'd like to donate a portion of the proceeds from every transaction to organizations that support women's causes, like homelessness, domestic violence, economic disparity. My clients would be able to choose which organization they'd like to support with the five percent of their sale. That way I'd feel that even if it's in a small way, I'm contributing something positive to others' lives."

He was at a loss for words. Which didn't happen often. Tasha's dream and selfless giving heart impressed him. "Wow. That's amazing."

"You know how people are always talking about changing the world?" Tasha asked. Her excitement was palpable.

"Yeah?"

"I've always thought that was so broad, kind of unrealistic for most people, really. But we can change *our* world. Our personal sphere of influence. That's what I aim to do. I believe it's part of God's plan for my life. However, it's a pipe dream right now."

"Why is that?" he asked.

"I've got a lot of debt. School loans and other stuff. All I need is a blessing." She finally paused and let out a nervous little laugh. "I'm probably boring you. When I'm passionate about something, I can go a little overboard."

"You're not boring me at all," he replied. A game plan was forming in his mind on how to pitch his idea to her.

"I'm sorry. I've gone on and on about myself. Blah. Blah. Blah. What about you? What do you do for a living?" she asked.

"I'm a professor and dean of the school of architecture over at Vista Peak West College."

"That sounds so interesting."

"Originally, when I went to college, I wanted to be a writer, but I've always also been fascinated with buildings and functional spaces where people live and work. So I switched to architecture. I was an architect for ten years. I liked designing things that were functional, sustainable, beautiful and ecological and a haven of sorts where people could live their best lives. I also liked the thought that long after I was gone, people would thrive and live out their lives and dreams in something

I created. Now, as a professor and dean, I get to ignite that dream in others."

"So your influence becomes exponential," she replied.

"I never quite thought of it like that, but yes, you're right," he said.

"Well, just always promise to use your powers for good," Tasha joked, her voice in a mock sinister tone.

He chuckled.

The restaurant buzzer went off, alerting them their table was ready. They were seated and reviewed the menu.

Tasha ordered the Hawaiian Surprise entrée—pancakes drizzled with caramel, pineapple and pecans. She told him how, growing up, her mom always made pancakes that were the size of a skillet for her on Saturdays, and when she'd first seen silver-dollar-size pancakes, she thought the restaurant cook had made a mistake.

"There was just something so special about those laid-back childhood Saturdays. The random sound of lawn mowers, kids playing, barking dogs—endless golden sunshine. Sweet times. I miss those simple times. I think we need more of those." She sighed. "Eating pancakes always brings that enchanted feeling back for me."

"Sounds wonderful," he said. He cut into his turkey sausage omelet and scooped up a healthy bite of the food. "I usually made my own breakfast." His temples tensed.

There'd been too many quiet mornings alone. His mother had often sequestered in her room, struggling with crippling bouts of depression from his dad's absences, and he'd been left to fend for himself.

He paused, as if trying to decide whether to say more. "I mostly ate cereal. If I wanted to switch it up a bit, I traded the regular milk for chocolate."

"Chocolate milk and cereal?"

He chuckled. "I was an interesting child, to say the least."

"You obviously haven't changed."

He gazed at her. "Should I take that as a compliment?"

"Most definitely."

He warmed at her kind words. Shaking his head several times to free himself of his contemplation of the past, he tried to figure out how to broach the subject of marriage with her. An idea came to him. "Tasha, question for you. Do your friends give you a hard time about not being married?"

"Uh, yeah. All the time."

"Mine, too. Ad nauseum." He whooshed out a long breath. "What if I told you I may have a way for you to make some substantial cash to achieve your business dream, as well as get your friends off your back about marriage once and for all?"

A flicker of concern flashed across her face, and he sensed her guard was going up. He got it. He was virtually a stranger and she didn't know where he was going with the conversation.

Zed gulped, as if readying himself to be submerged under water for a lengthy period, then uttered words he never thought he'd say. "I was thinking we could get married."

Chapter Two

Tasha sat stunned. What was going on? Had she been transferred to an alternate universe?

"Let me explain," Zed said. "I've got a beyond brilliant proposition for you."

She stared at him as if he were a Martian. "That much I got, Einstein."

His mouth curved into a half smile at her comment. "I have an idea that might benefit us both. Remember the Victorian where we met?"

She nodded.

"It belongs to my family."

She was even more confused. "*You* live there?"

"Yes, I once did."

"Why didn't you tell me?"

"It's a long story. You were a stranger. I never thought I'd see you again. I didn't consider an explanation necessary."

"And now you do?"

"Yes. The house originally belonged to my paternal grandmother, Gigi. She gave it to my parents as a wedding gift. My dad died unexpectedly of a heart attack when I was a teenager. Not too long afterward, my mom got sick. She put my aunt Zora on the house deed, too, in case something happened to her. Ultimately, it did. My aunt Zora died recently, and I'm the only surviving family member."

"So the house is yours now?"

He rolled his tea-with-lemon-colored eyes. "Not exactly. That's where you come in."

Tasha tried to connect the random dots of his conversation. It still didn't make sense.

"Here's the long and short of it. My aunt's will stipulated I can only have the place if I'm married. Otherwise, she's specified that it be sold to developers and torn down."

Tasha gasped. She couldn't imagine the lovely historic home no longer being there. The place had been special to her mother and herself. It would almost be like losing a small part of her own past, too. And the thought of the exquisite historic house becoming yet another razed property incensed her. It was unthinkable that the vintage gem might be replaced by some boxy, generic McMansion.

"There's more," Zed said.

Tasha massaged her tense temples. "Wait. Give me a moment. My mind's still reeling."

He covered her hands with his own. "I know. I'm sorry. It's a lot to take in."

They sat quietly for a moment, observing the animated holiday restaurant crowd.

"Here's the thing, Tasha," Zed finally continued. "My aunt and mom were hopeless romantics. Amazingly, my mom always believed in love, in spite of what she went through with my dad. Until their dying days, they wished for me to be married. They couldn't accept my decision that marriage wasn't a part of my plans." His eyes widened and resettled. "Like, ever." His lips formed a rigid, determined line to match his iron-clad declaration.

Tasha marveled that she'd stumbled upon yet another commitmentphobic man. It was like she was a magnet for these guys, or something. Not that it mattered anymore. *No, sirree. I'm good on my own.*

She had the Lord and she had great friends who were like family. What was that old saying? You couldn't choose your family by blood, but you could choose your family by heart. She'd done that. She didn't need anything else.

Tasha tried to ignore the sudden acid reflux that gurgled up in her chest.

Zed sighed. "So basically, the will's stipulation was Aunt Zora's last attempt at fulfilling their wish for me." He shook his head in apparent amazement. "Her intentions were good. I know she loved me." He momentarily stared at the sea of people around them. "Aunt Zora stated in her will that I could only have the place if I'm married for at least three months and live with my wife in the house during that time."

Tasha shook her head, as if to try to clear the thickening cobwebs. "Why three months?"

"She knew me. She figured I'd get a quickie marriage and annulment to get the title to the place. Which is exactly what I would have done."

"I still don't get the three-month thing."

"My aunt Zora was a bit quirky. She loved statistics and analytics. She was always quoting the statistic that it takes sixty-six days for a habit to form. She probably threw in the extra month for good measure. I think she figured if I lived with someone in the Victorian for three months, that it would allow time for something to possibly happen between me and my new spouse. I'm guessing she hoped I'd fall in love. She probably didn't want to force me to stay in something that I didn't really want, so if after the three months things didn't work out, I could still have the house and walk away from the relationship. But in her mind, at least I would have given marriage a chance."

He gazed at her intently. "Bottom line—I've got to be married to retain my childhood home, the residence that holds irreplaceable memories. A place I don't want to lose."

He paused. His shoulders heaved and dropped. He looked her way. "Neither of us wants a family. You want your own business. I want the house. I can offer you a lump sum that will help you financially meet your goal and accomplish your dream. You can help me save my house. And three months from now we can part, no harm, no foul."

Tasha attempted to wrap her mind around his words. In three months she could have the money for her long-held dream. Another part of her brain still thought the idea was like some chaotic Lucille Ball–like scheme. She and her mother had loved old *I Love Lucy* reruns. Tasha never thought she might one day live out a Lucy-like outrageous idea.

"I assure you, I would be a perfect gentleman. Separate bedrooms. We both can even do the whole background check thing. So you'd know you're safe."

Tasha observed this man who, twenty-four hours ago, she hadn't known existed. The wild thought hit her that she could actually live in the place she and her mother had dreamed of and loved since her childhood. She blinked hard, trying to clear her head of the roller coaster–like turn of events.

"Are you in, Tasha?"

She wrung her hands. "Zed, this is a lot to consider. I need some time."

He collapsed against his chair like a deflated balloon. "I guess you're right." He exhaled hard. "However, here's the thing—my aunt Zora set a time limit for me to marry, as well. I've dallied around, trying to figure out what to do. Now her deadline is looming." He peered at her, apparently gauging her reaction.

Tasha considered his aunt's plan. *Whew. Girlfriend had serious control issues.*

"I can make this very worth your time." Zed took out a pen from his jacket, along with a mini notepad. He tore out a sheet of paper, scribbled on it and handed it to her.

Tasha nearly gasped at the numerical figure he'd written. It was more than enough to get her business off the ground, pay off her bills and leave her with a healthy savings account to boot.

Zed retrieved his wallet from his pants pocket and removed a crisp white card with a university emblem embossed on it. "Here's my business card, with both my work and cell numbers. Text me your number. I need to know your answer within twenty-four hours."

Later, as Tasha took the southwest exit from Denver to Vista Peak, she considered Zed's proposition. She was still unsure how she would respond to him as she admired the first sight of her little town of Vista Peak, nestled just before the golden foothills.

She wound through downtown, past Avenue Parkway, until the ornate mansions turned into craftsman bungalows, then tiny modest homes. Finally, just before the small industrial section of town, she arrived at her neighborhood, a mixture of small apartment buildings and a mobile home park.

Her simple gray brick apartment building came into view. She parked and headed inside and up to her second-floor studio apartment. Milo, her cat, meowed loudly as she entered her place.

Tasha wiped her feet on the rubber grass-and-floral doormat, dropped her purse on her cherry-red chaise longue and searched for the cat.

She found him by his half-full silver bowl of food. His hazel eyes glared at her accusingly.

"What's up, you big baby?" she said softly, as if speaking to a child. And then she remembered. She'd skipped her daily ritual of feeding Milo by hand. Although he was more than able to feed himself, and usually did, this little additional snack ritual had become their habit and what he expected.

Tasha walked across the hardwood floor to the cat. She bent down and nuzzled his pointed furry chin. "You're spoiled rotten, you know that, right?"

Milo let out a half meow and rubbed against her black tights, leaving a layer of Day-Glo orange hair behind.

Tasha picked him up. "What am I going to do with you?" She reached into her mint-green kitchen cabinet for a paper towel and placed it by Milo's bowl. Tasha poured the food into her hand. Milo required a portion of his food to be hand-fed separate from his bowl.

Milo immediately went to work on his snack, his little mouth tickling her hand as he ate.

She took off her coat, flipped on the TV for the noise and plopped on her emerald green sofa-bed couch. She thought of Zed's proposition. "What am I going to do, Milo?"

Milo peered up at her from his feeding frenzy as if to say, "Me cat, you human. News flash, I don't talk. If you don't got that, we got worse problems."

She stuck her tongue out at him.

His tail popped up and slowly swished, as if he'd been offended. Head lifted high, he sauntered past her like the King of Siam. Tasha could all but hear his thoughts. *Bow down and worship, lowly peasant.* He jumped onto a windowsill, his eyes fixed in a laser stare, like a predator who'd found something. She supposed he'd discovered a critter of some sort.

Tasha considered the day's roller-coaster turn of events and Zed's proposition. Was she really even entertaining such an idea? "Milo the Wonder Cat, maybe I am losing it?"

Milo dully observed her from the window before attacking what was probably a very unfortunate insect.

Zed's idea was more than a little over-the-top. On the other hand, she'd be helping him save his beloved home—a place she loved, too. She'd also be able to pay off her massive debt and accomplish her business dreams. With her modest salary and huge debt, her dream was all but impossible.

But what would her mother have said? She'd had such an awe and reverence for the sanctity of marriage. Although her mother had never married, having become pregnant and abandoned as a teen, she'd always held the institution in high regard.

Would it be right for her to tarnish her mother's ideals by making marriage nothing more than a business arrangement? She could only imagine what her mother would have thought of Zed's scheme and of her living in their dream house.

Was she really considering marrying a stranger? Even if it was for just three months?

The marriage could help her in more ways than just financially. She'd been the singles' pastor at her church for four years, and she'd also been the wedding planner for many of these same folks' weddings. During her run, there had been more marriages than any other time in the history of the church. At her last meeting with the pastor and elders, they'd started by singing her accolades and noting her amazing accomplishments. She should have guessed it was the buildup before the letdown.

After their praise they brought up some concerns and gently challenged her. Apparently, others from the singles' group had relayed her sometimes snarky, critical comments about marriage when it came to herself.

She hadn't always been this way. But her heart had been mortally wounded on the battlefield of love. Whenever she'd loved someone and let her heart hope, her dreams had been cruelly dashed by unreciprocated love. Until she was just done with it all. So very done.

Tasha thought she'd disguised her less-than-stellar opinion about marriage for herself by veiling her comments in jokes. She'd evidently been wrong.

When she'd expressed her opinion to the pastors, they'd listened respectfully. She mentioned that regardless of her view on marriage for herself, she was a strong proponent of the institution for others.

After Tasha had finished speaking, Pastor Landry had looked at her with a mixture of affection and sympathy. *Tasha, you know we love you. We want God's best for you. We salute your amazing success in the singles' ministry. And if we thought you had a healthy view of marriage, this would be a nonissue. We'd like to pose a question to you for serious consideration. Are you really happy being single or are you running from marriage, and perhaps God's blessing for you, out of disappointment or fear? Only you can answer this question.*

She'd cringed at his words. Unexpected tears had sprung to her eyes. She hated crying in front of others, and she hadn't wanted them to believe her reaction proved their point.

Would she be denigrating marriage by considering Zed's option? Could she be true to her clients and the singles' group members, whom she encouraged to make a covenant commitment, by treating marriage so lightly?

Tasha shook her head, trying to clear the haze of confusion that clouded her mind. The one thing she did know was that she needed to make a decision—and fast. And what she decided could have a major impact on her life.

* * *

Zed unhooked his tie and twisted the key in the front door of his craftsman bungalow home. Before entering, he turned to admire the Vista Peak town square, just down the street. He could see the tops of a few of the early twentieth-century storefronts. The town view had sealed the deal for him on the place when he'd purchased it fifteen years ago. He liked that Vista Peak's older neighborhoods remained mostly intact, untouched by time.

When he entered his house, he slipped off his shoes in the black-and-white tiled entryway and hung his sweater on the hallway coat hook.

Heading into the living room, he admired the sheaths of angled daylight shimmering through the generous living room windows. He wasn't used to being home during the day.

Midmorning, he'd texted his secretary, Sheri, and let her know he was taking the afternoon off. Something he never did. He'd needed the time to go to Union Station.

Sheri had replied:

Excuse me. Is this an alternate universe? Has Zed Evans been captured by aliens and reprogrammed? Who are you and what have you done with my boss?

He texted her back:

Yeah. I know. It's not all play, though. Will work a little bit on the university building task force project.

He'd put off the task, knowing how politically charged the task force would be. It was being created to propose a possible campus redesign that might mean razing a beloved historic building, Lincoln Hall, which had once been the social epicenter of the campus.

Zed opened the blinds fully. Generous sunlight poured in, along with an amazing view of the Rocky Mountains, just west of Vista Peak.

He gave the mountain range different names, depending on how they looked daily. Today their rocky crags were a bold, deep blue hue. He dubbed them "Sassy."

Zed gazed around his place, pride bubbling in his chest. He'd had the home professionally decorated by one of Denver's top interior decorators. The place looked like a magazine cover and was no doubt beautiful, but sometimes it seemed a little impersonal to him. He wondered if that said something about him as a person.

His phone pinged, and he slipped it from his pocket. It was Sheri.

Take a break. Don't work 2 much on the task force stuff. Really take the day off. Smell the flowers.

In response, Zed punched in a smiley face.

Sheri's suggestion to *smell the flowers* for some odd reason made him think of Tasha. Based on her wistful story about coming to Union Station as a holiday tradition, she must be someone who stopped to savor things. Such as smelling the flowers. He was more like a speeding freight train—no time to ponder, always straining toward some new achievement or goal.

He headed to the kitchen and got a bottle of sparkling water from the refrigerator. Tasha was sweet, quirky, thoughtful and intriguing. And now she held a major part of his life in her hands.

Wariness engulfed him, like an early alert warning system. He didn't mind being friends with women, but that was all he wanted. In his experience, most women wanted more, even if they claimed to just want to be friends. Even when he gave them the 411 right up front, letting them know he wasn't marriage material and would never be, women often took his declaration as a challenge. They figured they could change him. However, they hadn't known his iron-clad stubbornness and determination.

If Tasha accepted his proposal, could she possibly have a change of heart after they were married? Could she become all clingy and hopeful that he'd want to be with her permanently?

He remembered the determined look in her eye when she proclaimed no interest in matrimony. It was a look he recognized—her steely resolve was similar to his own.

No. He was pretty sure she didn't want an emotional entanglement, just as he didn't.

His skin tingled under the sun blazing through the window, and he shook free of his reverie, laughing aloud at his thoughts.

He decided to follow his plan to get a little work done. Just as he opened the building task force folder and started to brainstorm potential faculty for the committee, his cell pinged.

Zed retrieved it and saw a text from Maya, his best friend Anton's wife.

Hey there, third wheel.

Zed chuckled at Maya's nickname for him. His usual lack of a plus-one often left him hanging out as a third wheel with Anton and Maya.

What up, what up? he texted back.

Anton got last-minute tickets 2 show at 7 at Red Rocks. Old-School Motown tribute. Thinking about dinner in Morrison B4 the show. Say about 5 p.m. Wanna come?

Zed flipped his thumb through the building task force files and figured he could finish a few objectives before joining his friends.

Sounds like a plan. As long as there isn't some unexpected honey coming that you're trying to set me up with.

He grinned even before Maya typed her response. He knew it would be funny.

Nope. Decided life 2 short to waste on worthless causes.

She'd added two smiley faces.

Smart girl.

Not 2 say that it isn't a shame that u won't let that rare diamond, known as your heart, be discovered.

He grimaced. Her kind words both surprised him and hit him like a brick.

He knew a lot of folks, but he was not known by many. Maya was one of the few people who had the uncanny ability to see past the walls he put up. Her discernment both excited and terrified him.

Thank you, Maya, he texted.

No. Thank u. 4 being u.

Because he knew Maya well, too, he heard the half snarky, half facetious tone behind the words, which the text couldn't translate.

Ah. You got jokes… Text details. Meet you there.

His thumbs paused as he waited for a response.

Okay, third wheel. Lookin' forward 2 rolling with u. C u soon.

Zed smiled to himself. He tried to imagine how his friends would react to the news he was getting married. Hopefully EMT services wouldn't be needed before he could explain everything.

Anton had been blessed to find Maya, though Zed had been skeptical when his friend first mentioned feeling different about Maya than any woman he'd known. When Zed saw it was true, he'd had to squelch some sadness and a little bit of jealousy. Anton had always been available to chill on a moment's notice. Until Maya.

But now the pair was like bread and butter. He was glad Maya had finally given up on finding butter for *his* bread. For the moment, anyway. Maya reminded him of the Energizer Bunny. She didn't give up too easily.

If Tasha accepted his unusual proposal, he'd need to introduce her to Maya and Anton.

He grabbed his keys, headed to his truck and wound through town onto the rope of crisscrossed highway leading to Morrison. He checked his watch as he rolled into the restaurant parking lot. After pulling into a spot, Zed gave himself a few moments to strategize how to bring Tasha into the conversation with his best buds. When he felt assured of his game plan, he headed into the restaurant. Once inside, he squinted, adjusting to the low lights in the place.

"Playa!" Anton's cry rose above the voices of the crowd. Zed grinned at the nickname his friend had dubbed him in college. It had been given more for his effect on the ladies than his technique with them. Though he could proudly admit he'd had game back then, too.

Zed followed the sound of his friend's voice and caught Anton enthusiastically waving from a corner of the room.

Weaving a zigzag path in between the tables,

Zed made his way to his friends. Maya, an enthusiastic hugger, popped up from her seat. She grabbed his shoulders and gave him a bear hug, then brushed his cheek with a kiss. "Hello, fine-as-wine-and-twice-as-nice," she teased.

When he disengaged from Maya, Anton was waiting. They performed a half hug.

"Thanks for the invite, dude," Zed said.

"No thanks needed, bro. Always happy to hang with my best bud and my lady."

Zed slid into the booth seat across from his friends, and Anton let Maya slide in before he sat back down.

"We ordered appetizers—wings, blue cheese and fried cheese sticks."

"Cool." Zed grabbed a menu and reviewed it. He decided on an Angus burger and O-rings.

The waitress appeared, loaded down with baskets of appetizers. Zed noticed her name tag read Lisa Cho. She gave him a shy smile and her dark eyes sparkled. "Would you like something to drink?"

"Sweet tea, no ice," he said.

Lisa nodded, as if making a mental note.

"I'm ready to order, if that's okay," he said.

"Sure." Her midnight-black straight hair swayed like a curtain as she retrieved her pen and pad from her apron.

He ordered, and Lisa added a wider smile

to her repertoire. When she left, he noticed his friends staring at him.

"What?"

Anton stretched out a fist for a pound. "Still got it, my brother," he teased in a high falsetto voice.

Maya observed him with a quizzical look. "Is there something you want to tell us?"

Zed looked between the pair. "What?"

"I called your office first, to tell you about tonight. Your assistant said you'd taken the afternoon off," Maya said. She gazed at him like an interrogating attorney.

"A guy takes a day off. So what?"

"You're not most guys, Zedrick Evans. You're a workaholic—on steroids," Maya said. She always used his full name when she was trying to make a point. "Something's fishy." Her dark eyes narrowed.

Zed let out a long breath. Had Maya just provided the perfect segue into bringing up Tasha?

Maya leaned forward, as if she instinctively expected a secret to be revealed.

"You guys might as well know—I'm getting married." He was speaking in faith that it would happen and it would be to Tasha. Zed braced himself.

Maya's eyes grew big. Her mouth opened, but

nothing came out. She looked from Anton back to him several times.

Anton looked concerned. "Honey, are you all right?"

She nodded and took a huge gulp of her water. While Anton appeared concerned about his wife, he, too, seemed shocked.

"Who? When? How?" Maya inquired in rapid succession.

"You're not even dating anyone," Anton declared.

"This isn't part of some TV reality show, is it?" Maya cried.

"Hey. Both of you, calm down." He told them of the will and his aunt Zora's unusual request. When he was done, they were still staring at him oddly.

"Okay, dude. I think the reality show thing would have been more believable. Your aunt was a character and a half," Anton declared.

"So who's the bride-to-be? Did you order her delivered by DoorDash?" Maya quipped.

"Nice," he responded. "I met her this morning."

"This morning?" Anton cried. "You met a woman this morning who has agreed to marry you for three months?"

"She hasn't agreed yet. I've given her twenty-four hours."

"How generous of you," Anton continued. "Who is she? What do you really know about her? Does she know about your inheritance from your dad and that you're loaded?"

"We haven't had the chance to get acquainted. And, no, she doesn't know about the inheritance. However, we'll have a prenup that keeps us both protected."

Anton gave his wife a dumbfounded look. "Maya, say something. Talk some sense into this man."

Maya leaned back against the booth. She crossed her arms, and an odd little smile curled her lips.

"Maya, baby, what is it?" Anton asked.

Her eyes sparkled. "Your aunt Zora might have been onto something."

Surprised, Zed stared at Maya. "I thought you said you gave up on me, as far as women were concerned."

"Seriously, dude, here's a little Girl 101 for you. No matter what we say, where love's concerned, for most of us, hope always springs ee-ternal," she replied, elongating the first syllable of her last word for emphasis.

Zed shook his head. "I have to admit Tasha's not like anybody I've ever met." Even if there wasn't a woman alive that he wanted to commit to long-term. Like. Ever. He vehemently vowed to never be like his father, who'd chosen his career as his first and primary love over family, breaking his wife's and son's hearts in the process.

"Aw, snap, dawg. Playa down," Anton cried. He collapsed against the seat, chuckling like a fiend.

"What part of 'this marriage is a business arrangement' don't you both understand? My mind hasn't changed about marriage and family," Zed insisted.

Anton shook his head in apparent amazement. "Bro, word of warning—don't underestimate the mojo. It can do things to the best of us." He wrapped his arms around Maya and gently kissed her cheek. "We often go down fighting, only to find when we land, we've gained something far greater than we ever could imagine. Is it scary? Yeah. Is it worth busting through the fear? No doubt."

Zed sighed. What Maya and Anton had was what he'd always wished for his mother. He couldn't count how many times, as a young boy, he'd sat with her watching sappy love stories on television. He'd often been bored to tears. After all, these weren't his beloved bromances, with explosions, harried car chases and fight scenes to the death at every turn.

He'd witnessed both raw yearning and sorrow in his mother's expression while they watched the rom-coms. What kept him going, and helped him endure the romantic movies, was the light in his mother's eyes when she watched a couple fall in love and have a happy ending. He'd longed for the same happiness for her.

Maya and Anton were his first examples, up close and personal, of true love in action. And Anton had been a hard-core bachelor back in the day.

Zed fought rampant emotions. Although he'd prayed and begged God for a similar love story for his parents, he'd seen his mother's heart shattered. He knew he'd been the only bright spot in her life.

Would God ignore his prayers now, too, to save the house that held precious memories of his mother and her fierce unconditional love for him?

His worrisome thoughts followed him through dinner, the concert and the ride home. When he arrived back at his house, he was weary. He put on his pajamas and headed to bed. But sleep eluded him most of the night. He tossed and turned, and in the morning, when he awakened, bleary-eyed from the late-night concert, he checked his phone. His heart dropped. No messages.

The longer he didn't hear from Tasha, the greater chance she wasn't going to agree to his plan. And time was running out.

Had he really proposed to someone? He'd

never thought he'd utter those four little words, a phrase that turned women to jelly, while often leaving men shaking in their boots at the gravity of it all.

He imagined Aunt Zora and his mother high-fiving each other and looking down from heaven with amusement.

The thought of his beloved childhood home being flattened to the ground distressed him. The place was more than a house; it represented the only time in his life he'd experienced pure, unconditional love. While his mother, Evelyn Evans, had her issues, loving him had never been one of them. The house was also partially the reason he'd become an architect. Even as a child, he'd appreciated the unique amenities and beauty of the place. He'd known how blessed they'd been, as a Black family, to live in such a grand home.

Tasha held the cards to his life in her hands. He groaned and inwardly chastised himself. It was his fault for waiting until his aunt's timeline whittled down to days. He had nobody to blame but himself. If Tasha refused his offer, he wasn't sure what he'd do.

He rechecked his phone for messages. *Nada. Zilch. Zero.* Realization hit him like a sledgehammer. He might really lose the house and something far worse—a link to the only happiness he'd ever known.

Chapter Three

Tasha awakened to slats of angled sunlight beaming on her face through the blinds. She blinked hard. Surveying the room, she found Milo in her laundry basket sprawled on top of a pile of clean clothes.

When she was finally fully awake, she remembered the previous day and Zed's proposition.

She sat up. The anxiety in the pit of her stomach was still there. She'd hoped that sleep would provide clarity. However, she was more confused than ever.

Her phone pinged, and she grabbed it from the side table. It was a text from Zed.

Need to talk. Can u meet me at the Copper Pot in the town square?

Tasha groaned. She was certain Zed wanted to gauge where she stood regarding his proposition. He might even try to influence her, if she was still hesitant. She reluctantly texted him that she'd meet him.

After tossing her phone on the nightstand by her bed, Tasha showered and prepared a light breakfast.

She didn't know what she was going to tell Zed, but she knew he was running out of time. It would only be fair to let him know something.

After her shower, Tasha checked her phone. Zed had responded.

C u there.

She quickly dressed in a Kelly green sweater, jeans and red Keds. After pulling her hair up, she put on her favorite black fedora, then added oversize silver hoop earrings to finish off the look.

She fed Milo before slinging her pink bedazzled combo backpack and purse over her shoulders and headed for the downtown square. She decided to walk, grateful for the forty-minute stroll to town to give her time to consider her decision.

No doubt, she loved the Victorian. Her heart went out to Zed. It was also true that she was stoked to think her dream of her wedding planning and venue business could become a reality. But marriage was huge. The real deal. If anyone knew this, she did. As a wedding planner, she'd witnessed love and marriage firsthand countless times.

Would she somehow hurt her wedding business by making marriage a for-profit business deal in her personal life? Her stomach twisted with anxiety when the town square and the ancient black clock at the center came into view.

Hoping to take her mind off things, Tasha admired the quaint square. Some of the redbrick storefronts had been there since before the turn of the twentieth century. Fresh flowerpots lined many of the buildings' windowsills. A curtain of white lights draped across the square in a rope of enchanting color.

The pretty scene lifted her spirits. "Lord, I really need Your help. I need to believe You've got me," she whispered as she walked toward the Copper Pot.

Zed was sitting outside the coffee shop, under a forest green canopy. He wore a camel-colored coat, khakis and white shirt. Tasha had to admit he was a beautiful specimen of a man. It was more than just his looks; it was the combination of confidence and kindness that was potent.

The wistful look on his face, a mixture of hope and fear, nearly did her in. She held his life in her hands.

"Hey," he said as she approached. He gave her

a friendly hug. "I already ordered a coffee. Hope that's okay."

"No problem."

"Can I get you something?"

"I always get the same thing—hot chocolate, extra whipped cream, with a pinch of cinnamon."

Zed laughed. "A pinch of cinnamon. How does one do a pinch?"

She grinned. "I don't know. They figure it out. I leave it to their interpretation." *Like I'm leaving it up to my interpretation whether it's a good or bad thing to turn our lives upside down with your wild proposition.*

Tasha took a seat as Zed headed inside the coffee shop. She rehearsed different speeches in her mind, weighing the pros and cons of her options.

Watching a stream of early risers leisurely stroll down the sidewalk, Tasha wished her future path were as easy.

The coffee shop door reopened and Zed exited, carrying a cup. He handed it to her as he seated himself.

"I hope your coffee didn't get cold while you were getting my hot chocolate."

"Oddly enough, I actually like lukewarm coffee," he said.

Tasha eyed her hot beverage, admiring the tall mountain of whipped cream speckled with cinnamon. She sipped the drink, licking the sweet cream off her lips.

Zed observed her. "Please tell me you've got good news for me."

Tasha took a tentative second taste of her hot chocolate. "That depends."

She saw the hitch in Zed's breath, evidenced by the jump of his Adam's apple.

"I want to help you, really I do," she said.

He sat up straighter, as if bracing himself. "Do I hear a *but* in your tone?"

Tasha peered at him. "Zed, you have to admit the idea is a little bit over-the-top. To say the least."

He picked up his beverage. Tipping back his head, he swigged the entire cup. Afterward, he one-shot dunked the empty container in a nearby trash can. "I guess this means your answer is no." She saw the defeat in his eyes.

Tasha quietly studied him. He was alone in the world. Just like her. They both were like wandering stars in the galaxy. Tethered to nothing. And the house was all he had left of his mother.

"I have an issue with it all," she admitted woefully.

Zed checked his watch. To her surprise, he abruptly stood. "Thanks for considering it. It was a lot to ask. It was nice meeting you." He reached out a hand to shake hers. Disappointment darkened his features.

Tasha mournfully shook her head. "I'm sorry, Zed. The thing is, the one issue is—with that felony in Illinois on my record, there might be a problem with the background check."

Zed's eyebrows hopped and settled. "What?"

It took a moment before realization lightened his sullen features.

She couldn't stop the grin that teased her lips. Since their first meeting, humor had been a connection between them.

They simultaneously burst into laughter.

"Does this mean what I think it means?" His light eyes scanned her face.

She grinned full-on. "Yes. I'm all in."

Before she realized what was happening, Zed let out a *whoop-whoop*, scooped her up and whirled her around. His strength and how easily he lifted and twirled her had her dizzy. Both literally and figuratively. *Get it together, girl.*

When he put her down, the tenderness in his expression nearly slayed her. "Thank you, my future missus."

Choked up, she was unable to speak, so she simply nodded. *What's happening to me?* She got herself together. "One thing. No offense, but I'd like to keep my name. It's too complicated to get everything changed, and it's not worth it since we're only going to be married a short time."

"No problem. I understand." Zed took a small notepad and pen out of his coat. He sat back down at the table. Tasha followed his lead and did the same.

"Okay. I'll need some information from you," he said. "We'll get the background checks started and we'll also have to get and file the marriage license. I'll arrange for us to meet with my lawyer to draw up a prenup, so you're assured you'll take away the agreed-upon amount we discussed and my financial interests will be protected. I hope that doesn't sound too callous."

"Not at all. This is a business deal. You have every right to have clear terms and to protect yourself. And I'd like to be protected and have it in writing that I'll receive what you've promised."

"Great. There is something else we must do."

"What's that?"

"You've got to meet my best friend and his wife. They're the closest thing to family I've got. Forewarning, they're not too happy that we don't know each other very well, even if this is a legally arranged marriage."

Tasha cocked her head. "We could remedy that a little and in a fun way."

"How so?"

"I could create a survey for both of us to take,

with questions about our lives. And then we could quiz each other on what we've learned."

"Quiz each other? Will there be a test?" he joked.

"Maybe," she said in a teasing tone.

"The background checks should take a few days," he said. "We'll meet my friends, and we can get married at the courthouse at the end of the week."

"I'd like you to meet my best friend, Kelly, too," she informed him. "She's in Europe, so we'll have to FaceTime."

"How do you think she'll take the news?" he asked.

"That, my friend, is the million-dollar question."

Tasha knew one thing. Kelly wouldn't hold back on her opinion about the matter. Her BFF had called her on the carpet many a time, believing she'd closed her heart to love out of fear. Would settling for a faux marriage for money prove Kelly was correct? Was she doing the right thing?

Zed parallel parked his truck in front of Tasha's small building, nestled in the north side of Vista Peak. The area was a mixture of modest homes interspersed with a few apartment buildings. It amazed him how the woman he hadn't even known existed had entered and changed his life in just three days.

The dying sun reflected honey-gold light off the windows as it melted into the horizon. He half walked, half jogged to the door and rang the doorbell. When Tasha buzzed him in, he climbed the steps to her second-floor unit.

When she opened the door, he stepped into the little studio with a hardwood floor in the living space and black-and-white tile in the kitchen area. Through the bathroom's open door, he saw a glimpse of pink tile walls and green fixtures. The place wasn't fancy, but it looked well lived in and loved, like it was her haven.

He was glad that in addition to the lump sum he promised her to start her business, he was able to pay three months of her month-to-month lease while she lived with him in the Victorian. She'd asked if he planned to rent out his home while they lived in the Victorian. He'd just casually said no, that he had that covered. He didn't tell her that finances weren't an issue for him, because of his dad's inheritance. Once he secured the Victorian, he'd sell his place.

Tasha gestured toward her cat. "This is Milo. I've made him promise to be on his best behavior and to avoid licking anywhere south of his chin. For now. At least, until he knows you better."

Zed chuckled. "Hey, Milo," he said. The cat gave him a dull-lidded stare.

"So this is my place," Tasha said, waving her hands.

"I like it."

"I'll take that as a compliment coming from a professor of architecture. It's kinda Bohemian chic. My best friend, Kelly, calls it 'everything but the kitchen sink' style."

"It's you."

"How so?"

"Quirky. Surprising. Category defying." The words that spilled out of his mouth surprised him. He'd been thinking them but hadn't meant to voice the opinion.

Her brows scrunched up. "Thank you. I think."

The cat rubbed up against his leg, leaving a layer of orange hair on his pristine, crisply pressed jeans.

"Sorry, he sheds a lot." Tasha picked up the cat and grabbed a pet-hair roller from a basket by the window. "You can de-cat with this."

He took the brush and patted Milo on the head before running the roller along his pants leg.

She grabbed a small plastic box filled with multicolored index cards.

"Cue cards. Really?"

"I told you there might be a test." Tasha lifted her chin proudly. "I'll have you know that I was a 4.0 student in high school and college because of cue cards."

"Okay, Professor," Zed quipped.

"Ah. You got jokes. But I plan to have a PhD in Zed."

Her statement caught him off guard and he realized Tasha's power to unexpectedly disarm him. He wasn't sure how he felt about her effect on him.

Tasha started to put on her coat. He went behind her and held the garment for her. "Thanks," she said.

He scanned her studio apartment again. Her place was certainly a reflection of her—a mixture of vintage and modern, contrasting colors and patterns and textures. Getting to know her was like the thrill of hunting for hidden treasure.

When they reached his vehicle, she turned to him with a surprised look on her face. "Wow, I'm impressed you parallel parked your truck on this street."

"What can I say? I've got skills. It's a gift."

"And so is your humility," she quipped.

"Ha ha." He opened the door for her and shut it behind her. After circling the car and climbing into the driver's seat, he started the engine and smoothly maneuvered the truck from the space onto the street.

"Quiz time," Tasha announced. She flipped a cue card. "What's the story about my father?"

He flicked on his turn signal and guided the truck into a main intersection. "There is no story. He was never there."

"Good." She started to turn the card.

"Wait," he said.

"What?"

"I want to know a bit more about that."

Her open expression closed. "Why? There's nothing much you can add to that."

Zed sensed there was more to the story, so he pressed through, wanting to know more about her. "Did they date and he abandoned your mom?"

Tasha's jaw tightened as she took in the view of the neighborhood's 1940s bungalows rolling by through the window. "My mom didn't like to talk about it much. Bottom line—he didn't love her. Or me."

His heart turned at her obvious pain. "His loss."

She blinked quickly and avoided his scrutiny. "Thank you. You were very blessed to have your family. And your amazing house."

He stared straight ahead. "Everything that glitters isn't always gold."

She looked surprised. "My mom and I always imagined a happy family lived in your home."

He bit his lip. "Sorry to disappoint you. If you like your version of my life better, go with it." He sighed. "Look, I don't want to make it sound like my parents didn't love each other. They did. In their own way."

He put on the brakes as a yellow light quickly switched to red.

She shuffled the cards. "Okay, let's move on. What's my favorite color?"

He thought fast. "When you were a kid, it was yellow. Now it's purple."

She grinned. "Wow, I'm impressed. Yours is pink because it was your mother's favorite. But you'll never admit that, for fear of your man card being rescinded."

"Good memory," he replied. "However, I'm going to let your implicit bias slide."

By the time they arrived at his friends' house, dusk was rolling its deep royal blue carpet over the sky.

Zed parked, jumped out and lightly sprinted around to open her door.

"Thanks," Tasha said as she got out. He watched her take in the nice ranch house, painted in two tones—chocolate brown and tan. Lights gleamed from several rooms. The yard, bushes and trees were well manicured. Rossdale, their neighborhood, was in between Tasha's place on the north side of Vista Peak and Avenue Parkway and Town Square on the south side of town.

"I'm nervous," she said.

"Don't be. They're going to love you."

As they climbed the front steps, the door swung open.

"Play-aaa!" His best friend grabbed him in a bear hug.

When they disengaged, Zed turned to Tasha.

"Anton, this is Tasha Jenkins. Tasha, this is my best bud, Anton Grimes. Anton and I have known each other since college."

"Nice to meet you. I'm a hugger. Can I give you a hug?" Anton asked.

"Sure."

Anton gave her a light, respectful side hug. "My wife, Maya, has been waiting by the window like a kid waiting for Santa. That's how I knew you guys were here before you knocked. Come on in."

A dark brown-skinned woman with a short afro greeted them inside. "Tasha! So nice to meet you. I'm Maya."

"Nice to meet you both. Zed speaks highly of you."

Maya's luminous brown eyes observed him. "That's nice. How funny. He hasn't told us much about you at all."

"Sweetie, be nice. Don't grill the girl the minute she comes in the door," Anton cried.

Tasha gave Anton a grateful glance.

"At least wait until she takes her coat off," Anton added.

Anton and Maya burst into laughter.

"All right, Frick and Frack. Enough," Zed ordered.

Anton's expression turned apologetic. "Sorry, Tasha. I was just playing with you. You'll soon learn that Maya and I are jokesters. In case you didn't know, Zed's a package deal. He comes with us. No refunds, no returns."

"I guess that makes me a blessed girl."

Pleasure warmed Zed's chest at her words. What was up with that?

He watched Tasha as she took in the home. He'd always liked Maya and Anton's homey furnishings, from the rust-colored L-shaped sectional that took up most of the living room, to the soft yellow walls and wall art, all in vibrant fall colors. A sixty-inch flat-screen television was positioned along the center wall, over a stone fireplace. A bright fire gently crackled and spit.

Scores from an in-progress football game rolled across the television screen, capturing his attention.

"Babe, why don't you turn off the game for a little bit. We've got company."

"But, sweetie, it's tied in the fourth quarter."

Zed saw the quick silent exchange between his friends. Sometimes he thought it was true that married couples could almost read each other's minds.

Anton switched off the television.

"Have a seat, you guys," Maya said, pointing to the couch.

He and Tasha obliged, and Maya and Anton sat across from them.

Zed enjoyed the light, friendly conversation his friends engaged Tasha in. Maya brought out snacks and beverages and seemed to take extra care in making Tasha feel comfortable. However, he knew his crew well, and it was only a matter of time before the light banter turned more serious.

After refreshing their beverages, Maya's dark eyes scrutinized Tasha closely. "So Tasha, I have to know what made you decide to follow Zora's wild plan?"

"In a word, money—it's all about the Benjamins."

Zed saw the quick look of worry exchanged between his best friends. While he'd explained his inheritance would be protected with their prenup, he guessed they might have thought Tasha was like a few of the ladies in his past who were gold diggers. While Maya wanted love for him, maybe she feared Tasha would hoodwink him into staying married, not out of love, but for his money.

He laughed nervously. He needed to lighten the mood. "You have to understand, Tasha's a jokester. You don't know her like I do."

"I guess seventy-two hours would give you an advantage," Anton quipped.

Zed stifled a chuckle.

"Maya, how did you and Anton meet?" Tasha asked, in an attempt to change the subject, he guessed. He could have kissed her. Or maybe not.

Maya's concerned expression softened. "We met in college." Her eyes glowed as she observed her husband. "I chased after him until he caught me."

Anton chuckled. "Ah, now the truth comes out."

"He wasn't used to a challenge," Maya continued. "The ladies fell at his feet like limp spaghetti. I liked him first, but I wasn't about to let him know that. So, I pretty much acted immune to his flirting. Drove him wild."

"I guess maybe that was my problem," Tasha said. "I never knew how to play the game. I wore my heart on my sleeve. And guys used my sleeve to wipe their mouths after they pretty much ate my heart for lunch."

"Oh, honey, while your metaphor is off the chain, I'm so sorry," Maya said.

"Thank you," Tasha replied.

Maya looked at him and back at Tasha. He saw the wheels spinning in her mind. And he didn't like where those wheels might be taking her thoughts.

"Tasha, don't give up hope," Maya declared.

Tasha tried to smile, but it fell short. "I think hope gave up on me."

Zed's heart turned at Tasha's words. He felt bad for her. Though Tasha had agreed to his plan and was going to benefit, would he end up becoming just another man who hurt her?

Chapter Four

Later, in the car, Tasha turned to Zed. "Did I say something wrong tonight? When Maya asked me about why I agreed to all this and I said money, you could feel the mood temporarily shift in the room."

"I'm sorry, Tasha. Maya and Anton are good people. They just love me. A lot. They're like family and very protective of me."

"Oddly enough, I totally get her fierce mama-bear attitude. I'd be the same way about my best friend. The money is important to me—you know that. But I sensed there was more to it with your friends, like maybe they were worried I was a gold digger or something."

"Even if that were true, the prenup will protect us both."

She decided to put her worries aside about the visit with Zed's friends and gathered her composure as Zed drove her home to repeat the same meeting with her friends. A glance at her watch showed it was almost eleven o'clock, which meant it would be almost six o'clock in London. Both Kelly and her husband were early risers, and Tasha was sure they would be up, most likely having coffee.

When they arrived at her studio, she hurriedly removed her brightly colored Christmas pillows and Milo from her couch for Zed to sit.

She took his coat and removed her own, hanging both on her wooden coat rack before joining him on the couch.

"Are you ready for this?" he asked.

"I think so," she said. Tasha was grateful that her BFF was out of the country. She'd known Kelly since middle school, and her friend would have lots of questions.

She'd already practiced fielding Kelly's questions, so she was semiconfident she'd be able to reasonably convince her friend that what she was doing wasn't a bad idea.

Zed sat on the love seat with her, obviously trying to keep a respectable distance, which was a little hard on the compact piece of furniture.

"Ready?" she asked. Zed stared at her, and her heart took off for an imaginary finish line.

"Do we need to discuss anything before the call?" he asked.

Tasha considered his question. "I think it best

to let me do most of the talking. You can just look pretty next to me."

Zed's deep chuckle filled the room. "I've never felt so much like eye candy before. Are you sure I'm not just your trophy?"

Tasha peered into the beautiful eyes she'd come to admire. "Welcome to how girls are often made to feel as soon as they hit puberty. Like our worth is directly correlated with our looks."

Zed's lighthearted expression turned serious. "For all us sometimes boneheaded men, I apologize."

His words both surprised her and turned her to mush. Who was this man? Afraid her feelings would show, she shifted her eyes from his. Pulling up Kelly's number on her cell, she hit the video call button.

Zed's arm slipped around the back of the couch behind her, and she could feel the warmth emanating from him. She involuntarily shivered.

"Cold?" he asked.

Just the opposite. Lord, help. "I'm okay."

On the third ring, Kelly answered.

Excitement trilled through her as her best friend's face appeared on-screen. "Kelly!" she cried. She truly missed her bestie.

"Tasha!" Kelly's phone went herky-jerky as it refocused on Kelly's husband. "Jaden, it's Tasha."

"Hey," Jaden said. His face appeared, with his

full brown cheeks, short hair cropped on the sides and fuller on top and beautiful smile.

"Where are you guys?" Tasha asked.

The camera swung back to Kelly. "Having breakfast on the veranda and waiting for sunrise."

"I'm so jelly," Tasha declared.

"Awww, honey," Kelly said. "I miss you!"

"Me, too." Tasha took a deep breath. *I might as well not waste time and just dive in.* "Kel, I've got news."

Kelly's dark eyes instantly narrowed with curiosity.

Tasha knew her friend had realized something major was up. Kelly had always been able to read meaning from the tone of Tasha's voice.

"What's up?"

Tasha had debated whether she should ease into her announcement, but she decided to go full throttle. "I'm getting married!"

Kelly's features froze in place. "Whoa! Wait— what? No way!" The video went shaky again as Kelly turned away from the phone's camera. "Jaden, Tasha's getting married!"

Tasha waited patiently. She knew her friend well. The serious reality of the situation would hit her soon. And then the interrogation would begin.

Tears spilled down Kelly's high cheekbones. "I feel like I'm dreaming! I mean, how…when?

I need details! Just a month ago, when I last saw you, you weren't even dating anyone."

Tasha was ready for the questions. She'd already rehearsed her response, like a lawyer stating their case in court. "Just so you know, Kel, this is a bit of a unique situation."

"How so?" Kelly said.

"Zed and I have a special arrangement."

"His name is Zed?" her best friend inquired.

"Sorry. In all my excitement, I can't believe I didn't introduce you first. Here he is."

Tasha swung the phone toward Zed, squeezing in so her image could still be seen, too.

"Hi, Kelly and Jaden." His tone was warm and extra gracious.

Kelly wiped away fresh tears. "Nice to meet you."

Tasha told her friend the story of meeting Zed and their three-month arrangement. When she was done, she observed her bestie and her husband. They both looked stunned.

"Kel, I know you're probably in shock," Tasha hurriedly said.

"To say the least," Kelly said. "I guess when I thought of this day, I expected to be overjoyed for my BFF, sharing in her happiness at finding love and a man who adored her. I thought of giggles together, planning the wedding, listening to you waxing lyrical about this man who could corral the stars and tame the sun—all for you."

Touched, Tasha pressed her hand to her chest. Would she be selling herself short by marrying Zed on his terms?

Jaden leaned into view. "Okay, guys. What's done is done. Let's cut to the chase. When's the big day?"

Tasha's heart hitched. "We're getting married this week."

Jaden's jaw dropped. The phone swung back to Kelly. "Wait, what?" she cried.

"The will stipulated a deadline for us to be married," Tasha sheepishly announced.

The silence on the other end was ominous. Kelly's happy expression turned concerned. She saw her friend look to her husband and then back at the phone. "You guys, please don't take this wrong. Zed, Tasha's my homegirl. She's like the other half of my heart. I love her. This is just all happening so fast."

The waterworks from Kelly started up again. Jaden patted her cheeks dry as Kelly composed herself. "Tasha, I don't mean to be negative. You must admit it's a lot to take in. I guess the bottom line is that I've got to trust you. You're a grown woman. Sweetie, I just hope you're not giving up on the real thing someday. And have you thought how this arrangement might affect your singles' ministry? People might think you have a callous, cavalier attitude toward marriage if you get divorced so soon after tying the knot, since they won't know about the arrangement."

Tasha's pulse ricocheted. Kelly's concern about her not giving up on the real thing was years too late. That ship had sailed, buoyed by the winds of rejection. As for Kelly's second point, Tasha hadn't thought about that. But it didn't matter now, because she'd made up her mind and given Zed her word.

She started to speak, but Zed gently squeezed her hand. "Let me," he mouthed. He gently swayed the phone toward him. "Kelly, I agree that we've thrown a bombshell your way. And then we acted as if you should just accept us rocking your world. I'm truly sorry for that." He looked at Tasha. "You've known this lady much longer than me. Where I think we can agree is that she is beyond incredible. I promise you, she will be safe with me and I'll protect her reputation."

Kelly's eyes stared intently through the screen. Her husband hugged her, his face resting against her shoulder. "I'm not going to lie, Zed," Kelly said, "this is hard to process. However, I trust my friend's judgment. At the end of the day, you're both consenting adults. And you've made your decision." Kelly paused. "Tasha, I love you to the moon."

"And beyond," Tasha added, repeating their favorite phrase.

"Where are you guys getting married?" her best friend inquired.

Tasha looked to Zed before she answered. "The courthouse." She winced, awaiting Kelly's response.

Kelly started to speak, but Jaden interrupted her.

"We wish you guys the best. Don't we, honey?" he said. When Kelly didn't answer, he repeated the statement.

Kelly looked resigned, but she nodded. "Hey, guys. We've gotta go. We signed up for an early yoga class. Love you, Tasha."

Tasha blew a kiss to her friend. "Me, too."

The phone beeped and the screen went dark.

Tasha's heart felt sore. Even if their relationship was fake as a Hollywood tan, their ceremony was going to be the real deal. It saddened her that her BFF wouldn't be at her side for moral support. Especially since Kelly would surely never have the chance to see her walk down the aisle again.

"How you doing?" Zed asked.

"Not so good." Tasha rose and went to her front window to watch the moon rise like a proud queen.

She heard Zed come up behind her. "You were amazing with your friend. I know it wasn't easy."

Tasha kept her back to Zed. She didn't want him to see her tears. There was a time she'd incessantly dreamed of her wedding day. She'd never imagined her life would come to this—a marriage that was a transactional business deal.

What was it about her that made her unworthy of real love and commitment? It was a serious question she had for the Lord.

Zed sat at his kitchen table and pondered the events of the past week as he watched the line of blue-gray morning clouds suspended over the mountain range. He folded the *Wall Street Journal* he'd just read. Tightening his robe, he rose to make another cup of coffee, adding milk, a couple of teaspoons of sugar and a pinch of cinnamon—a new addition, thanks to Tasha's hot chocolate recipe. An unexpected smile spread across his face at the thought of her.

His phone buzzed, alerting him he had an email. Opening the new message, he saw their background checks had cleared. Zed chuckled, thinking of Tasha's joke about the felony in Illinois. He forwarded the results to her, and shot her a text in case she didn't read her emails frequently.

He retrieved his laptop and grabbed a pen and

pad. There were four days left before the deadline Aunt Zora had established for him to be married, so they'd have to be married in the next few days. Uncomfortable with the idea of sliding up to Aunt Zora's final deadline day, in case something unexpected happened, he checked Vista Peak's county clerk information to see what they needed to get done.

He jotted down task notes. Thankfully, his classes were over for the semester and his dean duties were lighter, due to the university's shutting down for the holidays.

The Victorian was already furnished, but since Tasha would be moving into it with him, he imagined she might want to bring some of her things to make it feel more familiar. He'd need to schedule a mover. And he needed a new suit for the wedding.

His phone chimed. Anton's name gleamed on the screen. He accepted the call. "What up, dude?"

"We got it like that, right? I mean, you're my boy, and we're always straight with each other, right?"

Zed's heart skipped a beat. "You know it, bro."

"I like Tasha. A lot. But have you thought about your arrangement from another perspective—what if she falls for you? With what you've been through before with women thinking that they could change your mind about marriage, have you thought about that?"

"I appreciate your concern, but it's all good. Tasha's as adamantly against marriage as I am. That's one of the reasons I pitched the plan to her. I knew things would be safe with her and messy feelings wouldn't get in the way. And we'll have a prenup that protects us both financially. We also share similar faith and morals, which means I can trust living in close proximity for three months. To put it simply, she's perfect for my aunt Zora's imperfect demands."

"So when's the big day?"

"Probably Tuesday."

"Well, okay," Anton slowly declared. Zed heard the surprise in his tone. "Am I to assume our invitation's in the mail?" he quipped.

"Anton, dude, you do understand this isn't real? I mean, yes, we're really getting married, but it's just an arrangement."

"I get it, man. But you might as well know Maya's got it in her mind this might be some sort of poetic justice—getting you, who never planned to marry, down the aisle—for some greater purpose. And if this thing turns real, she will hate having missed the big day."

For once, Zed was happy that fate would help him. "I know. But she's got the big art show that day. And you've got the holiday thing at school with the kids." Maya, a museum director, had been working over a year on the museum's signature event and annual fundraiser. And Anton was head of Vista Peak Middle School's big holiday jamboree.

"Oh, yeah. Right. Couldn't you guys pick another day?"

"We want to be married before Christmas. And the date works best for us. Plus, we have the deadline."

Zed heard Anton sigh. "All right, playa."

"And you can tell Maya not to get her hopes up about some kind of love story happening. I promise you this marriage will have an end date. I haven't changed my mind about marriage." He paused, sipping his coffee. "And I won't do so."

"Just one more thing," Anton said with resignation in his voice.

Zed held his breath.

"Congratulations, bro."

"Thanks, man," he replied. When he hung up, Zed tried to get Anton's admission of Maya's hopes about him and Tasha out of his mind. There was no way he was going to cave in. He already had his first love—his career—and there wasn't room for anything more. He was glad that he knew himself well. Sudden heartburn gurgled in his throat. He ignored it.

Chapter Five

～

Tasha gazed at her reflection in the Vista Peak courthouse bathroom mirror. She fought back tears. It was her wedding day, but it was nothing like she'd once dreamed. Instead, it was the beginning of a marriage that was as fake as snow on an LA movie set. How had she gotten here?

She pressed her hand to the cool petals of the camellia positioned behind her right ear. It had been her mother's favorite flower. Its deep blushing-pink hue contrasted nicely with her vintage knee-length dress, covered in cream-colored macramé lace over silk. She held her arms out, admiring the wide sleeves that expanded like wings.

Even though her and Zed's relationship was nonexistent, it was a reality that she was soon to be a bride. For that reason, she'd chosen her dress with care. She admired her bright teal high heels. They added a much-needed pop of color, sass and spice to her outfit.

She peered heavenward. "Lord, I hope You see my heart in what I'm about to do. It's not just about the money, but about helping Zed save his home—a house we both love that's so much more than brick and mortar. And, Lord, I promise to do good things with the money I get from this. I will sow into the love story of others, through my wedding business. That's got to stand for something, right?"

Tasha stood still, almost as if she expected God to audibly answer.

Her phone pinged, and her best friend's name gleamed on the screen. Tasha's heart leaped. She answered. "Kelly!"

"Tasha, sweetie!" Kelly declared.

Tasha thought of the time difference in London. "Hey, what time is it there?"

"Don't worry about that. I couldn't let my girl go down the aisle without knowing my love and heart are with her."

Tears welled in Tasha's eyes. She grabbed a paper towel and quickly patted the tears away, not wanting to mess up her makeup. "Don't be silly. Remember this isn't real, girl."

"The courts would beg to differ," Kelly said.

"You know what I mean."

"Of course I do, hon. It's just that we've always been there for each other through everything and I want you to know that I've got your back. Always." Kelly paused. "Actually, I've been thinking a lot about things since your call. I want you to hear me out. While your unusual arrangement is over-the-top, to say the least, and at first I was worried you might have been settling for less than you deserve—I've started to wonder if this could be a blessing in disguise."

Tasha heaved a sigh. "Kelly, I love you, to the moon and beyond, but understand—this marriage is strictly a business deal. For the three months. It will end. Period. Please don't project your hopeless romantic feelings on this." She attempted to compose herself. "I've accepted that happy endings don't happen for me." She tried to ignore the tremor in her voice.

"Oh, sweetie, I know your heart has been broken and life has knocked you down. But the only way you can lose is by not getting back up again. You can't control what life throws at you, but you can control how you respond to it."

"Kelly, you know I love you. And I know you love me. I appreciate your call and your support. Really, I do. I'd better be going."

"Blessings to you, my friend," Kelly said.

Tasha swallowed hard. "Thank you." She ended the call.

Closing her eyes, Tasha let the quiet envelop

and calm her. "Here we go." Her lids fluttered back open. She strolled toward the bathroom exit, her high heels clacking against the tile floor as she admired the restroom's Art Deco curved glass wall.

Upon exiting the restroom, she found Zed leaning against a marble pillar. His smile broke the serious lines of his face.

He looked like a walking magazine ad in a navy blue suit with a purple shirt and matching tie. For a quick moment she considered the saying that the groom shouldn't see the bride before the wedding. Then she remembered it didn't matter. This was a business agreement. It would end.

Zed strolled toward her, looking at her like he was pleased at what he saw. "You look amazing."

Shyness overcame her. "Thank you. You clean up pretty good, too."

"Hang on. I've got a surprise for you."

Tasha stood as Zed lightly sprinted behind the pillar. He returned with a bouquet of flowers.

"Zed, they're lovely."

He studied her. "Every bride deserves flowers on her wedding day."

Every bride deserves to be loved and adored by her groom on her wedding day. The rogue thought escaped before Tasha could censor it. She'd said this to countless brides. Yet, here she stood, marrying a practical stranger.

"Are we doing the right thing?"

Panic streaked across his face. "You're not reconsidering?"

"I still see marriage as sacred. Even if it's not for me," she said.

"I get that. I feel the same way," he replied.

Tasha held tears at bay. "Am I cheapening the institution by marrying for money?" She heard the exasperated high-pitched tone of her words play back in her mind.

Zed held out his hand. "Come with me."

Tasha took his hand and let him lead her to a marble bench in a corner.

"Tasha, I need to tell you something."

He motioned for her to sit and he joined her.

"My family's house is more special than you know."

Her brows knitted in curiosity. "How so?"

"My great-grandparents were slaves. My grandpop was the first free man in our family. He fought in World War II. Despite the racism he faced, he was proud to defend his country. A decorated war veteran, he came home and couldn't find decent work. But he was determined. He worked three jobs. Nightly, he'd walk home, so dog-tired he could barely see, and he always passed the Victorian."

Zed paused as a young family, parents and a toddler, walked by. The parents held multiple

Christmas-decorated shopping bags. Once they passed by, he continued.

"A white family lived here with their twin sons. Sometimes my grandpop would just stop and listen to the sounds of the kids' laughter or the family talking while watching television. He was like a kid outside a candy shop, and he dreamed of raising a family in such a fine place.

"He met my grandmom, Gigi, on a blind date not too long after he returned from the war. She was sweet as pie, kind, funny, smart. However, she was not beautiful. Guys never got past her looks. She was considered an old maid, and my grandfather initially wasn't attracted to her. But he decided to make the best of it and be a good sport. He pretty much put her in the friend zone, and that's how he got to know her—her wit, intelligence, compassion, kindness. And one day he realized this woman had bowled him over. His love for her lit a fire in him."

"What a wonderful love story," Tasha declared. How his grandparents met and married sounded like something out of a movie.

"I know, right?" Zed replied. "They were soon married. All they could afford was a rudimentary clapboard tenement. But Grandpop had big dreams and he was a praying man. He wanted nothing but the best for Gigi. He told her one day they were going to live in the grand Victorian and that they'd have the life they deserved, like the white folks that lived there.

"Gigi would just laugh, figuring it was a nice dream. But unknown to her, he was putting away money. One night he was sitting in his usual place, admiring the house, when a drunk driver missed a turn. The car jumped the curb and hit my grandpops. Killed him instantly."

Tasha gasped, blindsided by the shocking turn of events in the story. Her heart instantly ached for Gigi. She could only imagine the woman's grief. "Oh, Zed, how awful!"

Zed paused. Tasha watched his Adam's apple bobble as he swallowed several times, obviously trying to rally his emotions. He finally continued. "Before he died, they'd been trying to have children. My grandmother had three miscarriages. Two months after his death, she found out she was pregnant."

"Seriously?" Tasha clasped her hand to her heart at this news.

"I know. Amazing, huh? Six months after his death, the family that lived in the Victorian moved. She started out renting the home, because African Americans were unable to buy homes at that time. She put away my grandpop's life insurance and the settlement from the accident, until she was able to purchase the house.

"When she moved in, the first thing she did

was plant a little garden of flowers around the tree where my grandpops used to sit. It's still there to this day. She always said God had given her the house and that it was the house that love built. Throughout Vista Peak people knew Gigi's house was a welcome haven. Black kids, white kids, Asian and Hispanic kids all came in and out of the house, filling up on my grandmother's love. She never married again. However, even though she only had one child, she was a mother to countless kids. Quite a few of their kids and grandkids have come back to see the place over the years."

"Oh, wow." Tasha wiped away tears. "That's a beautiful story." She gathered her thoughts. "And I know it's supposed to make me feel better about what we're doing. But it's just the opposite, Zed. It makes me feel worse. Like we're making a mockery of their true love and what the place symbolizes."

Zed clasped her hands. "Tasha, I get what you're saying. But I don't see it like that. The house is their legacy of love and desire for a better life. Sometimes I feel their blood, sweat, tears, hopes and dreams are absorbed in the plaster and the very foundation of the place. By saving the home, I feel we're honoring and keeping alive their legacy."

"When you talk about that legacy, Zed, it makes

me wonder why your aunt would put the house in jeopardy to be sold to developers and demolished if you didn't agree to her little plan."

"As much as my aunt loved the house, she loved me more. She never had kids of her own. I was like a son to her. She was stubborn and wanted a loving family for me, especially after what my mom and I went through with my dad. She made the stakes high, to force my hand and to let me know she was serious about me at least giving marriage a try. She knew me well enough to trust I'd fight to keep the house."

He stood and held out a hand. "Are we gonna do this thing?" he said softly.

A memory of her first act of bravery—jumping off the diving board at thirteen—came to mind. She'd finally closed her eyes, pushed away her fear, and without thinking, she'd leaped into the unknown. Tasha recalled the mixed feelings of terror and exhilaration she'd felt. It was much the same right now.

Zed observed her with laser focus.

She rose and took her future husband's hand, and they headed for the judge's quarters.

A woman with a name tag that read "Lois," wearing a tweed pantsuit, with stiff 1980s high hair, greeted them when they entered the office. She admitted that she was a sucker for weddings and offered to stand in as a witness, even though it wasn't necessary to have one in Colorado. Her gray eyes sparkled with warmth.

The judge was different. His monotone voice said he'd done this too many times to count and just wanted to get it over with.

Tasha was surprised at her swirl of emotions. Although she knew their relationship wasn't real, it would be legal. She stared at the handsome man across from her. His good looks were the thing romance novels were made of. And in minutes she was going to be his wife.

When it came time to exchange rings, Tasha placed the simple gold band she'd purchased on Zed's finger. Then he took something from his jacket pocket.

She gasped when she saw the ring. It was a lovely vintage, obviously expensive, ring.

"It was Gigi's wedding ring," he whispered as he placed it on her finger.

"Zed," she whispered back, "it's too much."

He shook his head. "She, her love and the house are a big part of all this. This ring makes it like she's here with us."

To her surprise, the ring fit perfectly. Before she realized it, the short, perfunctory ceremony was over. And the judge was telling Zed that he could kiss his bride.

She hadn't thought about the kiss. How could she have forgotten about the kiss?

From the deer-in-the-headlights look on Zed's face, he hadn't considered it, either.

Lois and the judge observed them expectantly, and Tasha knew if they didn't do something soon, it would make things even more awkward.

Zed moved toward her, his eyes silently apologizing. He lifted her chin with his finger. Her breath hitched at the surprise of the soft, full warmness of his lips. His kiss was tender, yet tentative, and she felt dizzy. To steady herself, she reached for him, clutching his suit sleeves.

He drew her closer for a second before his mouth disengaged. And an involuntary whimper escaped her at their abrupt separation.

His lips slid to her ear. "Thank you, Tasha," he whispered.

When he stepped back, she could see that his eyes glistened. He quickly swiped his eyes.

Lois broke the awkwardness of the moment. "Awww, I love it when the groom cries. Gets me every time. He obviously really loves you." She swatted at her heart with her hand.

Tasha rallied her emotions. Lois's sincere words only made her feel more like a fraud. What had she done? She gazed at the man across from her, who was now her husband, signed, sealed and delivered.

When they exited the building, Helen Jennings, Vista Peak's senior librarian, and Anita

Lane, from Nita's Trinkets downtown gift shop, were walking by. They noticed Tasha's bouquet.

"My word, Zed Evans, is that you?" Anita cried.

Helen peered up at the sky. "Has the sky turned purple, Nita? Are aliens on the way? That's tantamount to Zed Evans taking a bride!"

The women burst out laughing.

Zed smiled. "I guess I deserve that."

The women congratulated them. The conspiratory glance they gave each other as they walked away alerted Tasha that news of her marriage to infamous confirmed bachelor Zed Evans would travel through town faster than the internet. Nevertheless, she sensed their genuine happiness. That was one thing that Tasha loved about small towns—most people were genuinely overjoyed for others' happiness.

At the bottom of the courthouse stairs, she and Zed peered at the emerald green esplanade across the street. Multiple food trucks were splayed across the lawn. Clumps of people were gathered around the mobile food units. A jazz band was stationed in the pristine white gazebo in the middle, and music filled the air.

Zed turned to her. "Well, my temporary wife, would you like to go somewhere to eat to celebrate?"

Although she knew he was joking, it still hit her. She was somebody's wife.

She viewed the food trucks. "I'd give my right arm right now for a fully loaded hot dog—onions, relish, mustard, a dollop of ketchup." Her love of junk food was something she rarely admitted. When she had done so in the past, many of her ex-boyfriends had berated her. Their criticism had been everything from being critical of her ingesting white flour and carbs from the buns, to one ex who called hot dogs "chemicals wrapped in skin." Secretly, she'd once longed for a guy who could be silly and sometimes eat junk food and love it.

Zed's eyes sparkled. "You forgot green peppers and a dollop of hot sauce. Then, and only then, can it be truly classified as fully loaded."

Tasha scrunched her nose in delight. "You don't mind?"

"Mind? Seriously? I'd race you there if I didn't have on these ridiculously fancy-pants shoes."

Her half snort, half chortle escaped her lips like an errant prisoner. Embarrassed, she observed Zed. His expression was not critical, like those of others who had heard her unusual cackle.

They strolled over to the esplanade and each ordered loaded hot dogs from one of the booths. A cool breeze rippled through the naked winter branches as they walked and ate their hot dogs.

Tasha couldn't remember when she'd last had so much fun. She liked how Zed could be serious and carry an intelligent conversation, as well as just chill. They finished their meal in record time, then listened to the band for a while.

"Think we should go check on Milo?" Zed finally asked.

She thought of her four-legged baby, tucked away in his carrier in the oversize Victorian. He was probably confused and frightened. "You're probably right. Thank you for thinking of my baby."

They walked a few blocks to where his truck was parked. Zed gently blocked her from harm, while he watched for traffic on the busy one-way street. Once it was clear, he opened the truck door for her. She gently placed her bouquet in the back seat as Zed jaunted around to the driver's side and entered the vehicle.

They buckled up, and she helped him make sure the way was clear before they pulled out onto the historic brick road. They navigated the roundabout and its focal point—a historic statue of a white settler, a Native American man and an African American man, their left arms all lifted in the air, their hands joined. The monument honored the unique history of the town, which had deep influences from the heritage of all three men represented.

Tasha snuck a look at her new husband, his silhouette highlighted by the backdrop of the town, decorated for Christmas. She felt she was living in some holiday romance movie. But this was all too real. And there wouldn't be a happily-ever-after.

When Zed's vehicle pulled up to the Victorian, he heard Tasha's breath swoosh out. He kind of got her reaction. The house was easily one of the most beautiful in the neighborhood, especially with its holiday decorations.

He parked in front of the place, rather than in the two-car garage in the back. Before Tasha could get out, he leaped out and came around to get her door.

"My missus," he said. He grinned and extended a hand to her.

She grabbed the skirt of her dress for an apparent tasteful demure exit. "Thank you, my mister," she replied, taking his hand as she climbed out of the vehicle.

He took her coat from the back of the seat and draped it around her shoulders. "Ready?"

Tasha sucked in a huge burst of air. "Yes." He knew how momentous this was for her, living in the place she'd dreamed of since childhood. She followed him through the black iron gate, down the historic red stone pathway. The white wooden steps creaked under their weight as they climbed them.

At the top of the steps, Zed opened the intricate lattice-trimmed screen door, then twisted the key in the ornately carved wood door with a beveled glass face. He paused and turned to her.

"What?" she asked.

"Are we going to keep with tradition? This is the threshold, after all."

"Seriously, Zed? Nobody's watching us now. We don't have to front."

"Yeah, I know. But we both will never do this again, right? Would it hurt to do a little of the tradition for fun?"

Her expression turned quizzical. "You put marriage and fun in the same sentence. Have you fallen ill?"

"Humor me." He held out his muscular arms.

Tasha gazed at him. "Awww. Is this from the playa-play ego handbook? Even though this is all make-believe, are you mentally beating your manly man chest, even if it is in mock conquest?"

Her comment caught him off guard.

"But then again, what would it hurt to be carried over the threshold like a real, adored bride? I'll never do this again. Thankfully."

He swooped her up in his arms.

A car motor sounded on the street behind them. Turning with Tasha in his arms, he spotted an elderly couple in a pristine vintage gold Cadillac. The pair observed them.

"Oh, Merle, to be young and in love," the woman said breathlessly, her voice high-pitched and winsome, carried by the winter breeze.

Zed guessed Tasha heard the comment, too.

Reality gut-kicked him. This wasn't real. The boat-size Cadillac slowly glided away.

The fun of the moment escaped him, like liquid through a funnel.

Tasha peered at him. "What's the matter?"

"I'm fine. Sorry. I shouldn't have been playing around." He put her down on the plush, thick Persian rug in the foyer. He saw her eyes roll over the hallway's rich wainscoting and Anaglypta wallpaper.

"Wow. Just wow," she declared. "I never get tired of admiring your house's amazing details."

"What are some of your favorite things?" Zed asked.

"Oh—that's hard. There's so much. I love the grand Z-shaped staircase, the foyer fireplace with the green marble tiles and the stained-glass window halfway up the stairwell. I also absolutely love and adore the pocket doors leading to the dining room."

Hearing a high-pitched meow, Zed went into the adjoining dining room and through a swinging door to the butler's pantry, then returned with

Milo in his carrier. The cat's irises were large black orbs, which covered his naturally hazel eyes.

Tasha hurried toward the carrier. "Hi, baby," she said, greeting the cat.

Zed unlatched the carrier, and Milo shot out and ran straight for Tasha. She lifted her furry baby so he could nuzzle his orange-and-white face against her.

Zed could hear Milo's purr, like a low generator rumbling from his chest.

"Thanks for letting me bring Milo."

"I wouldn't have had it any other way."

She stared at him. "Is it really about Milo, or more about the fact you'd do anything to save your place?"

He clutched his hands to his heart in mock angst. "I'm not heartless, Tasha. Although I care about my home, I care about you and what makes you happy, too."

"I'm sorry. It's just been my history with men that they'd do or say anything to get what they wanted. In my experience, altruism has not been a common trait among the opposite sex."

"We're not all like that, Tasha."

She looked like she wanted to press his point but decided against it.

"Let me show you your and Milo's room," he said.

She followed him upstairs, and he led her into a sitting area that contained a rose-colored sofa and a high-back chair with matching accent colors. A door with filmy lace curtains covering its glass led to the home's turret.

"This is your room." He pointed to the first bedroom off the sitting room, which had the best light from its western position. Rather than vintage furniture, it had a modern bed, small love seat and twin chest of drawers. "This was my room, growing up," he said. "It's my favorite place in the house."

She shook her head in protest. "I don't want to take your favorite spot."

"No worries. The place has plenty of good spaces. I'm staying in what used to be my dad's office." Sadness pinged his heart at the statement. His dad hadn't been home much to use his office. He'd spent countless hours in the room, daydreaming his dad was there and they were doing various father-son activities. "Back in the day, it was a smoking room for men to chew the fat and talk about the news of the day. It's farthest away from your bedroom."

"May I ask where your parents' room was?"

He kept his expression neutral. "They had separate rooms. My mom was a light sleeper and dealt with headaches and depression. When he was here, he usually slept in one of the spare rooms. My mom was in the room next to yours." He stared into the room, loneliness socking him in the gut. He missed her terribly.

"I can tell you were close to your mom," she said. "I miss my mom, too. I wore her favorite pearl necklace today. As a way to have part of her with me." She pulled the delicate strand of pearls from under the neckline of her wedding dress to show him.

Zed studied the necklace. "It's beautiful."

"It's kind of plain," she said. "But my favorite part is what she said about it—that a pearl's beauty comes from constant friction and agitation. Even though we have hard times, if we let Him, the Lord could make something beautiful out of it."

"It's a nice saying," he replied.

She observed him. "But you don't believe it."

"I'm just thinking of the sand that goes through all the agitation and friction. I'm sure the sand's not thinking of beauty in the midst of the pain." He loosened his tie, remembering his mother and her long suffering over his dad's treatment. "It's been a long day," he said. Fatigue caused his voice to sag. "If you don't mind, I'm going to take a shower and chill."

"Are we doing anything special for Christmas Eve tomorrow?"

Although the conversation about his mother

brought a wave of sadness that made him want to isolate himself, he didn't want to make her holiday a bad one. It was her first Christmas without her mom. She didn't deserve him being morose and depressed. She'd also agreed to this odd scheme to save his house.

"Let me sleep on it," he said. He tried to give her a reassuring smile but knew it fell flat.

After he helped her bring in some of her things, Zed retired to his makeshift bedroom. He tried to get some work done on the building task force charge, but after a while the text on the computer screen started to swim. That was when he knew it was time to give up on catching up on work and just go to bed.

He had a feeling he wouldn't sleep well. The topic of his parents had brought on the familiar sadness and bewilderment over their relationship, feelings most acute during the holidays. While anyone looking in from the outside would have thought this was a happy home, that wasn't the case.

He'd heard his mother's bitter sobs more nights than he cared to remember. And to be honest, he'd hated how she'd given his father so much power over her. It was like a line he remembered from an old movie. The heroine had woefully proclaimed that "she couldn't live" without the love of her life. While it sounded impossibly romantic, he disliked the remark. He didn't think anyone should have that much power over someone. He was even more disappointed with his pops for choosing his career over his family, especially his wife.

Despite his history of mostly woeful Christmas holiday experiences, he did enjoy celebrating the day set aside to honor Jesus, God's greatest gift to the world.

He gazed out the window at the darkened sky, sprinkled with glassy stars. Milo lay in a furry clump at his left foot. For some reason the cat had become enamored of him. He could only pray that Milo's owner wouldn't do the same.

Chapter Six

Tasha awakened and was startled. She blinked hard at her unfamiliar surroundings. Then memories flooded her. She was married and living in the purple Victorian she and her mother had loved.

She stretched luxuriously and drew the warm covers around her. The high, narrow windows let in beams of morning light. Admiring the stained glass that topped the trim of each window, Tasha resisted the urge to pinch herself.

Gentle snowfall made the scene outside look like a giant snow globe. The smell of bacon and coffee wafted into the room, along with festive music.

Tasha climbed out of bed and put on her fluffy pink robe and matching house shoes, then headed to the bathroom across from her room to wash her face and brush her teeth. After rebraiding her hair, which had come loose during her night's sleep, she considered putting on lip gloss but decided against it. Sooner or later, Zed was going to see her without makeup. He might as well get over the shock now. Tasha chuckled at the thought.

Milo's carrier door was open and the cat was nowhere to be found. She'd noticed Milo appeared to have fallen instantly in love with Zed, so her pet was probably with him. Even though she was the one who had rescued him from the animal shelter, fed and provided a home for him and loved him. *Traitor.* She refused to agree with the animal's assessment of Zed's charms.

When she finally headed downstairs, Tasha followed the aroma of coffee and bacon to the kitchen.

Zed was in an Ole Miss T-shirt and striped gray sweats. His massive arms nearly popped out of the sleeves. She saw what looked like the beginning of a tattoo peeking just below the sleeve over his left arm. He was barefoot and stood by the vintage stove, stirring something in a skillet.

With surprise, Tasha noted a stack of perfect gold pancakes on a plate on the kitchen table. Flowers in a crystal vase added a pop of color against the white lace tablecloth.

"Mornin'," Zed said.

She tightened her robe belt, although underneath she wore full pajamas. "Morning."

"Did you sleep well?" Zed asked. He sprinkled some sort of seasoning in whatever he was cooking.

"Pretty good. Although, I was kind of confused when I first woke up."

"Ah, new environment. I get it. That happens to me a lot, especially when I stay in a hotel."

The heat registers softly whistled. Tasha saw her traitor feline, formerly known as Milo, at Zed's feet. Milo was cleaning his paws in between staring adoringly at Zed as if he were the sun, moon and stars.

"I hope you're hungry," Zed said.

She laugh-snorted. "Is that a trick question?"

He smiled, awakening his dimples. Removing the skillet he was working on from the burner, he turned off the fire. "Before we go further, I'd like to apologize if I was a little moody last night. Holidays are a mixed bag for me. Even so, it wasn't fair to dump my emotional baggage on you."

She nodded. "Thanks for saying that. I get the holiday thing, too."

Tasha saw the question in his eyes at her statement. She debated whether to be more specific. The kindness in his expression and his humble apology made her decision for her.

"I have the dubious honor of having been broken up with on three holidays."

Zed looked surprised.

"I know," she continued. "It's some kind of weird record. First, I was dumped on Valentine's Day and left to pay the check at a five-star restaurant. Then there was the time I was unfriended on Thanksgiving, as well as uninvited to my boyfriend's house for the occasion. The last holiday breakup was by Christmas card. Sort of like a kiss and a slap. Merry Christmas, loser." She paused, her throat tight. "It's kind of ironic that on days meant for celebration and feeling loved and special, I was made to feel anything but that. Sometimes I used to wonder, was it me? Was something wrong with me?" She was embarrassed to hear the quiver in her voice.

Zed winced. "I'm so sorry, Tasha."

"Thank you." She bit her lip and fought the emotions that bubbled within her.

Zed picked up the skillet from the stove and headed to the table. She saw fluffy yellow eggs with flecks of red and green peppers, mushrooms and onions. Zed scooped the food onto two festive, holiday-themed plates.

"Since the holidays hold challenging memories for us both, maybe we can replace some of those bad memories by doing some fun things. Today we can do stuff we loved to do as kids. Even if it's totally off-the-wall. Like eating Froot Loops for dinner, staying in our pajamas all day, watching cartoons, stuff like that. Whatever you want. Tomorrow we can have a traditional Christmas. Most grocery stores sell holiday meals. I could pick something up for us. What do you think?" Zed asked.

Tasha kept her face blank, but inside she felt all squishy. Who was this man who could be so thoughtful and kind? Why would he limit himself from having a family? She started to think maybe she understood a little of what his aunt Zora and his mom had seen in Zed that made them wish for a different life for him.

"Sounds really cool," she responded. Mentally, she shook herself free of her thoughts about Zed. Yeah, maybe he was an amazing guy. But she couldn't get that confused or put on rose-tinted glasses about him. The man didn't want a family. Ever. And it wasn't fair for her to try to fit him into any other idealistic mold in her mind. She'd been there, done that with other guys. And it had always led to disaster. She needed to honor who he said he was and what he wanted. But what would be so wrong with suspending reality for a bit and enjoying the season?

She had a husband for three holidays. Christmas, New Year's and Valentine's Day spanned their agreement time. *Why, he's my holiday husband.* The thought nearly caused her raucous laugh, snort-style, to escape. But she imprisoned the urge, safely locking it in her throat.

"All right, then, great," Zed replied. "After breakfast we can make a formal Christmas Eve wish list for what we'd like to do today." His eyes rolled over her face. "The sky's the limit, little missus."

Tasha's heart flipped at his acknowledgment of her as his wife. She tried to maintain a poker face. "I have one request now."

Zed scooped the last bit of his eggs onto a golden-brown piece of toast and consumed it. "And what would that be?"

"Can we play Christmas carols? My mom and I always loved holiday songs."

"Easy-peasy," he said. "We wired an amazing sound system in the house a few years ago. I'll program some Christmas music for us."

After Zed got the music started, he helped her load the dishwasher with the breakfast dishes.

When they were done in the kitchen, he started a roaring fire in the living room fireplace. As if on cue, featherlight snowflakes began to fall more steadily outside.

Tasha went to the front bay window and sat on the window seat. The winter scene outside was beyond lovely to her. Some kids across the street danced in the snow. Then they stood still, raised their faces to the sky and gleefully held out their pink tongues to collect falling flakes.

She felt warmth behind her and smelled a hint of cologne. Zed had joined her to watch the outside scene, as well.

"Oh, for those carefree days again," he said wistfully.

Tasha nodded in agreement. A few vehicles drove up slowly, blocking the view of the kids. One vehicle was an SUV and the other was a green station wagon. Each were loaded with people. They stopped in front of Zed's house. The vehicles' occupants stared at the house, their mouths forming perfect oval shapes as if they were amazed. Tasha recognized the mixture of awe and wonder in their expressions. It was the same way she and her mom had felt each Christmas they'd stood in front of the home, looking at the grand house and beautiful decorations.

Was she really sitting here, at Christmastime, in her dream home? She laughed to herself at the wonder of it. Instinctively, she waved at the carload of folks. To her surprise, they excitedly waved back.

She watched the car drive pass and then turned to him. "What's your favorite Christmas memory?"

Zed crinkled his brows in deep thought. "I can't think of a specific one. I guess the few times where my dad was home. He was a railroad exec when I was little. Later, he worked for the airlines. He was gone a lot." He stared out the rapidly frosting window. "I just wanted to be like the other kids and wake up Christmas morning with my dad and mom, and open presents and act silly while they watched with pride and love. Mostly, it was just my mom and me. She'd give me my gift from her and my dad. Though the card with the gift was signed from both of them, it was always in her handwriting. My father usually called us from wherever he was at, but it wasn't the same." The sorrow filled his eyes, turning them into fathomless pools as his gaze connected with hers. "What about you? What's your favorite Christmas memory?" he asked.

"Honestly, it was coming to this house. It was always the highlight of our year. It's like the enchantment of this place promised endless possibilities—that dreams might really come true someday."

He sighed. "And now I've tainted those memories for you."

Tasha shook her head. "No, you haven't. Not really. I mean, yes, I'm sorry to hear that your home wasn't as happy as I'd dreamed it was for the family that lived here. Even more so, now that I know you. But in a way, that's the blessing of Christmas. The gift of Jesus brought light and beauty to our dark world."

She stood and turned to face him. "God's still in the business of answering prayers, Zed. Although my mom didn't have much, she always said she was rich in the ways that were most important. She'd found the true joy of Christmas. Even in her darkest circumstances, she clung to that joy. So my greatest holiday memories are visiting this house and experiencing my mother's childlike faith and simple joy during the holidays." She paused. "As much as I love reminiscing and I've always been nostalgic, I just hope and pray that my future holds wonderful experiences just waiting to happen."

Zed observed the colorful glittering tree in front of them as he pondered Tasha's favorite Christmas memories. "I wish my mom could have had your mother's hope and sense of wonder about things. It would have made things a lot easier for her. I don't think she would have been so dependent on my dad to fulfill her every need."

He had a sudden desire to make the day wonderful for Tasha. And beyond that, he determined that for every holiday they were together, maybe he could make memories for her that would replace her sad holiday experiences. That would be his gift to her. Something about her made him want the best for her and gave him the need to bless her.

"I have some ideas for today," Tasha said with a smile. "Let's watch vintage TV shows, roast marshmallows in the fire, eat our fave childhood meal—mac 'n' cheese and hot dogs for me, which I noticed you have in stock—along with whatever you'd like to do, and at the end of the day we'll have hot chocolate by the tree. Instead of reminiscing on what we didn't have, at day's end we can thank God for the good things we did have in our lives. Although I know it was hard with your dad being gone so much, there must have been some good things that you loved about him, too, right?"

He nodded, amazed at this woman. "Who are you, Tasha? I've never met anybody like you."

She raised her chin at his words. "And you won't again. So you'd better take advantage of these three months you have me," she joked.

He could tell she expected him to laugh. But the comment struck an unexpected chord in his heart, leaving him speechless.

Zed peered out the window as another car drove up and slowed by the Victorian. This time he didn't wave as he often did. Suddenly, pretending didn't seem quite as fun anymore.

"What's wrong?" Tasha asked.

Zed tried to shake his mood. "It's nothing. Really."

Tasha scrutinized him. "All right, mister. No sad faces allowed for the next twenty-four hours. Let's go." She grabbed his arm.

"Where are we going?"

"You'll see. Just get your coat."

Zed obeyed. Tasha led him outside. "It's perfect," she said as she peered out at the blanket of snow. "Down on the ground," she ordered.

"What?"

Tasha ran into the yard, found a space in between the decorations and collapsed. She waved her arms and feet. "Snow angels."

He laughed. "C'mon, Tasha. I'm a grown man."

"Maybe that's your problem." She flicked a curtain of snow at him.

He chuckled and reluctantly joined her, finding a spot and gingerly lying down. Surprisingly, looking up at the sky, the joy of gazing at the stars as a kid came back to him. He started to slowly move his arms and legs. With each movement he started to go faster until he was laughing aloud with childlike abandon.

When he was done, he noticed Tasha was watching him, an impish grin brightening her features. He stood and dusted himself off. He gazed at their matching angels.

"You missed a spot," Tasha said. She gently

dusted snow off his left shoulder. Her touch was as light as a feather.

"Okay, we have to give them names," Tasha said. "Mine is Serefina."

"I like it," he responded. "It sounds like an angel's name, delicate and sweet—" He started to add "like you" but decided against it.

"Thank you for the compliment. Now, what's your angel's name?"

He squinted his brow in thought. "Tasha the Great."

Tasha's eyes widened before she burst into gales of laughter. "Really? She's kind of a husky angel, huh?"

He observed her. "Show my girl some love. She's got strong shoulders to lighten others' burdens, carry their prayers and bring them joy." His gaze connected with her eyes until she looked away.

At the end of the day, after Tasha had retired to bed, Zed sat by the fireplace, satiated by the dying fire. Outside the living room window, a white marble moon and crystal stars shimmered in the sky. The day's storm had blown through.

He was glad for some solitary time to reflect on probably the most interesting Christmas Eve he'd ever had.

They'd completed all of Tasha's wishes for the

day and his, too. She'd endured his childhood favorite meal of bologna on Wonder Bread, with grape jelly. In addition to watching old vintage TV shows, they'd watched his favorite holiday movie, *It's a Wonderful Life*.

During their final hot chocolate and reflection, he'd recalled the things he loved about his dad. He'd admired his father's intelligence, quick wit and the way the man knew so many random, useless facts. Which had made him hard to beat at trivia games. When Grant Evans poured on the charm, he was hard to resist. Maybe that was what had made him a successful executive, too. Zed realized he could acknowledge that although his father was a workaholic, the man had given him and his mom a great life, in terms of material things. There were Black families that would have longed to have the life he'd been blessed with.

When he'd finished telling Tasha these things, her soft brown eyes had sparkled. She'd said she was proud of him for being vulnerable and opening up to acknowledge the good things about his father. He'd resisted the urge to preen like a proud peacock.

I think you've just started your journey toward healing, she'd finally declared.

Her declaration had stayed with him long after their time together. Now he finally stood and stretched, then grabbed the fireplace poker and dabbed out the final dying embers.

His eyes fell on a photo of Aunt Zora on the mantel. Zora wore one of her elaborate, high-church hats, with a smart, fitted, peach-colored suit. Her taupe skin glowed, setting off her amber eyes, only slightly darker than his own. Her oil-black hair spilled around her shoulders, and her smile set off her full cheeks. He marveled at how much she resembled his mother. The only difference was that his mother's eyes were lighter, like his own, and she had high, sleek cheekbones that dipped into sunken valleys, rather than Zora's chipmunk-full cheeks.

Zed wondered when his aunt had cooked up the marriage scheme. Why couldn't she have just given him the house? Hadn't he been through enough drama with his dad's bad behavior, and the untimely deaths of both his parents?

The stairs creaked behind him, and he turned to find Tasha had returned downstairs.

She had a determined look on her face. "I think we need to go to Union Station for Christmas tomorrow. You need to face your feelings about the place and the holiday, full on. Once and for all."

Anxiety made his stomach gurgle. He wasn't used to being called on his fear.

He watched Tasha's eyes widen in surprise. She must have seen the distress on his face. He wasn't used to being vulnerable. Putting a wall of steel around his heart had been the best way to protect himself from his father's emotional blows. In his childhood world, he'd learned vulnerability opened you up like defenseless prey.

"You won't be alone to face it. I'll be with you," she said.

Now it was his turn to be surprised. Warmth splayed across his chest like sunbeams. He gazed at the diminutive woman across from him. Her kindness and ability to see beyond his walls to his heart touched him. That wasn't something most people could do, or took the time for, beyond his best friends. It made him want to give her the world even more—to replace her sad holiday experiences with happy memories, even if he just had three months and three holidays to do it.

Chapter Seven

Tasha's body ached from lack of sleep after tossing and turning most of the night. She wasn't used to waking up groggy on Christmas Day.

Even Milo, who usually was with Zed, must have sensed her anguish. He'd jumped on her bed and stayed by her side the whole night. He'd even endured her fitful twists and turns, which usually agitated him and made him scurry to more peaceful quarters.

Christmas Eve had been so wonderful. She couldn't remember the last time she'd had so much fun.

The intimacy she and Zed had experienced in doing their dual silly and serious tasks had emboldened her. Her intuition, along with Zed's hints about his past, had helped her string together some things about him, including the reasons for his aversion to Union Station. The vulnerability and fear in his eyes had nearly done her in.

Tasha wondered if that was part of the reason Zed kept to himself. Maybe he'd never had anyone close enough to him to call him out on his stuff. While his protective mechanism of isolation kept a wall of safety around him, had it also kept him emotionally stifled because he didn't deal with his issues?

She climbed out of bed. Milo shot from on top of the covers and headed for his pet bed, evidently upset his sleep had been interrupted.

Tasha showered and dressed before putting on her favorite emerald green silk dress pajamas and diamond post earrings her mother had given her for her eighteenth birthday.

When she went downstairs, it was quiet.

Bright Colorado sun poured diffused light through the draperies. Tasha opened the living room and kitchen curtains and started a pot of coffee. She liked that Zed didn't have a fancy-pants coffee maker.

While the coffee percolated, she scampered out onto the porch and grabbed the newspaper. Although it was cloaked in thick orange plastic, it was coated with snow.

She observed the quiet holiday morning scene, peering again at the place where she and her mother had once stood, taking in the house. Tasha looked heavenward. "Merry Christmas, Mama," she whispered.

After bringing the paper in, she placed it on the kitchen table, along with an empty mug for Zed for when he awakened and decided to come downstairs.

Tasha retrieved the box of Froot Loops, of which Zed had consumed three bowls on Christmas Eve during their fun challenge. She hoped repeating his pleasurable meal from the day before might bring him joy again.

Pouring herself a cup of coffee, she doctored it with cream and sugar to her liking, then headed to the tall Christmas tree. Some of her holiday glee returned as she observed the gifts beneath the tree.

An envelope-size gift, wrapped in gold tinsel and adorned with red-and-green ribbon sat on top of the pile. She picked up the odd present. Her name, in Zed's large, generous handwriting, was on the card. She put down her coffee mug and unwrapped the gift.

There were three greeting cards inside. A folded piece of notebook paper sailed from the wrapping and danced to the floor. Tasha retrieved the note.

Tasha, these three cards are for three new holiday experiences to hopefully replace the mem-

ories of your three holiday breakups. Merry Christmas. —Zed.

Tasha cupped her mouth in surprise and awe.

She heard rustling upstairs and realized Zed was awake. Her hands shook as she hurriedly rewrapped Zed's gift to her and tossed it back under the tree.

Tasha ran upstairs, then headed to her bedroom closet and removed an art book from her luggage. She'd made pencil drawings since childhood. When she was twelve, she was pursued by an art school. But she decided she preferred to sketch as a hobby, rather than something she had to labor at as a career.

Her fingers flipped through the art tablet, fanning the pages until she came to the special drawing for Zed. She'd worked hard on it from the day she knew they'd be married and together for Christmas. It was a drawing of Zed as she imagined he must have looked as a small boy at Union Station. He was peering up lovingly at someone. Since she didn't know what Zed's dad looked like, she'd just drawn a man's strong hand at the top left edge of the picture. The large hand was holding Zed's small one. He was looking up adoringly at his father, his young face beaming. Tasha prayed Zed would like her gift because she'd poured her heart into it.

Pride swelled within her. "Thank You, Lord. Because of You, this is one of my best works."

She foraged farther in the closet, until she found the frame she'd purchased. Putting in earbuds, she listened to Christmas carols as she framed and wrapped Zed's gift. When she was done, she pressed her ear to her bedroom door. She heard water running in the bathroom across the hall and figured Zed was in the shower.

Carefully carrying the large picture downstairs, Tasha propped it up against a wall by the tree.

She nestled herself in one of the plush living room lounge chairs. Through the bay window, she viewed the front yard. A tickle agitated her throat. "Mama, I'm here. I'm really here. Living our dream." Emotion overcame her.

Various memories of her mother's life crowded her mind. Her mother's wistful expression whenever she saw couples walking hand in hand. Mornings when the garish fluorescent kitchen light highlighted the harsh lines etched in her mother's face. Her mother's expression deepened by worry, as she balanced her checkbook. Even with her mom's faithful coupon hoarding, the woman had squeezed every penny she could out of her meager pay for them to get by.

Tasha was blessed with a better life because of her mother, whose hard work, encouragement and belief in her had given Tasha a better foundation to start her life on. And it was her mother who'd discovered the Victorian, as she walked to the bus after the nearby housecleaning job she'd taken on to supplement her income.

When Tasha had first met Zed, he'd wondered if her mother's prayers from heaven had brought her to this place. While she wasn't exactly living the real fairy tale, she was going to be blessed with a better life because of Zed's offer. And she'd be able to bless other people's love stories through her wedding planning and venue business. But why was she always the one on the sidelines, watching others' happiness? Was God mad at her?

Tasha shut down her pity party before it got started. She had learned to love and treasure herself, and just because treasure wasn't discovered, didn't mean it wasn't treasure.

In a way, it was as if the house was her and Zed's fairy godmother. The structure, grand dame of the neighborhood, had sheltered, embraced and blessed her and Zed.

Zed. Just the thought of him made her smile. She loved their cheesy jokes and humorous banter with each other. He was such a good guy.

Tasha grabbed a pillow and hugged it to herself. A part of her wished she could be like Cinderella, and the ball would never end. *Careful, girl. Remember, if you're Cinderella, midnight's coming, and there's no glass slipper for you.*

"I need to be the prince of my own life," she whispered to herself as she leaned back in the chair and closed her eyes.

The next thing she knew, a curtain of daylight seared through her eyelids. She awakened to bright sun.

Tasha ran her hand over her right cheek. The imprint from the living room chair had made indentations that snagged her fingers. She ran her hands through her matted, kinked hair, where she'd slept against the chair. She didn't want Zed to see her like this. Especially not on Christmas Day.

As if on cue, Zed descended the stairs, followed by Milo.

"Merry Christmas, Tasha." His light eyes glittered with warmth.

Her breath hitched in her throat. The thing that made him so devastatingly handsome was that he didn't know it. Even in casual clothing, he looked like he had stepped out of a media ad. Now that she knew the man, too, that made him even more lethal.

A strange feeling came over her. In anguish, she started to wonder why she'd been given this opportunity to get so close to a good man like him—the kind of man who had never been available to be hers and never would be.

She straightened in the chair. "About last night. I'm sorry. I hope I didn't overstep my bounds with the Union Station suggestion. It's like I read the first page of the book of your life and acted like I knew the whole story. I shouldn't have presumed."

Zed nodded. "As you've figured out, it's a sore spot. Thank you for the apology."

Tasha breathed a sigh of relief. She was happy the air was cleared between them. Her best friend always told her that a big part of marriage was compromise and forgiveness. And giving the other person room to be themselves, in a safe place. Is this what Kelly had meant?

She noticed Zed looking toward the kitchen, probably thinking about breakfast.

"I don't know about you, but for me, opening Christmas gifts always trumped breakfast," she declared.

Zed slapped his forehead with his hand. "What was I thinking? You're right."

"We can eat later," Tasha said.

"Deal," he replied. He took her elbow and gently guided her toward the tree.

They both stood there for a moment, enjoying the beauty of the tree and the backdrop of the enchanting outside scene through the window. The houses draped in glittering Christmas decorations were highlighted by a light sea-blue sky and coating of pure white snow.

"You go first," she said.

"All right." Zed rubbed his hands together excitedly. His eyes went immediately to the large gift she'd brought downstairs. He retrieved it and tore open the wrapping.

Tasha tried to suppress her combination of excitement and anxiety. She hoped she'd done the right thing. When Zed fully unwrapped the gift, he froze. He looked from the drawing to her and back at the present. "What?" he managed to eke out.

Tasha's pulse raced. Had she made a mistake?

Milo sat next to Zed, looking at the framed picture of Zed as a young boy at Union Station.

"I can't believe what you've done," he said.

Her heart dropped. "I'm sorry. I didn't mean to upset you."

Zed put the picture down and approached her.

Tasha braced herself for an earful of his displeasure.

His hands gently clasped her shoulders. "You don't understand. It's as if you looked inside my soul or something. Your drawing expresses how I always wished it would be with me and my dad." His Adam's apple bobbed and settled several times. "Thank you, Tasha."

Turning back to the tree, he grabbed the envelope that she'd secretly already opened. "Merry Christmas." He handed it to her.

Her honest nature got to her. "I have a confession to make. I already opened it."

"I may not be able to forgive you for that," he announced.

Surprised, she started to protest.

Zed laughed outright, his severe declaration an obvious joke.

Relieved, she chuckled, too. "Your gift was so thoughtful. I love the idea of three good holiday moments to replace my three holiday breakup memories. You don't know how much that means to me." A mixed soup of emotions swirled within her.

"Tasha, are you all right?"

She reined in her emotions. *Get yourself together, girl. Remember the playa-playa handbook. Men are experts at playing the game. It's not about the prize for most of them, but about their competitive nature and winning. The game is the thrill. When they've won, they move on and leave you like a quickly discarded Christmas toy. It's about conquest. They're all alike.*

"Yeah, I'm good," she replied.

After they finished opening gifts, Zed made Christmas pancakes. *So much for Froot Loops,*

Tasha thought. However, she was just glad he was making a meal that made him happy.

He used frozen red strawberries for the Santa hat and lips, whipped cream for the beard hair and hat rim, chocolate chips for the eyes, and a pat of butter for the nose.

"Wow, I'm impressed," Tasha said when she saw the special breakfast.

"What can I say? I got skills," Zed joked. He headed to the refrigerator. "Want some milk?"

"Sure."

After pulling two glasses with Christmas elves on them from the cupboard, he retrieved a jug of milk and poured twin glasses.

Tasha's toes curled in satisfaction as she enjoyed the pancakes and the serene Christmas morning. She liked that she and Zed were comfortable not always needing to talk. That they could be quiet and just enjoy things. Most of her past boyfriends hated silence. They always had to be talking, listening to something or watching something. As if they were trying to avoid alone time with just themselves.

Zed devoured two stacks of pancakes and drank three glasses of milk.

Tasha laughed as she viewed his empty plate. "It's not a race, you know."

He gave her a wide grin. "I've got one last surprise."

She shook her head in confusion. "What?" She put her fork down.

"There's one more gift for you." Zed sprang up. But instead of heading to the tree, he went to the foyer closet. She heard him rummaging through something. He returned with an old shoebox. It was dusty and dirty and wrapped with a single, dingy ribbon.

She crinkled her nose. "You shouldn't have. Really," she said, looking at the tattered box.

"Don't judge a book by its cover," he said.

"Well, that's not a book, it's a battered old shoebox. Therefore, all bets are off."

Zed chuckled. He sat down across from her and caressed the box with his hands, as if he held treasure. "My aunt Zora left this. For you."

Tasha's head snapped back. "I don't get it. How could your aunt Zora leave me a gift? She didn't know me."

"She left it for my wife. The one she knew I'd have for at least three months. Thanks to that unusual eccentric will of hers." He slid the box across the table. "Actually, I was as surprised as you when my lawyer gave it to me. Aunt Zora stipulated it was only for my wife to go through."

Tasha eyed the box. "Your aunt Zora was a character."

"Ha. If you only knew," Zed said. Affection beamed from his eyes. "She didn't just walk to the beat of a different drum. There was no drum where she walked."

Her hand teased the ribbon, gently pulling at the crooked old bow. But she didn't want to open it. Not in front of Zed. If Aunt Zora had meant it for her, she wanted to open it in private.

"Hey, I was thinking maybe I'd like to go to Union Station like you suggested," Zed said.

All thoughts of the box flew out of her mind. "Really?" Had she gotten through to him? Was he possibly ready to start his journey toward healing? He was such a good guy. His mom and aunt Zora had known that. And now she did, too.

"Let's do this thing," she said.

True to his word, later that afternoon, they headed to the city and Union Station. A brisk wind whirred and danced through Denver's downtown corridor of buildings. Zed was surprised to find a moderate amount of people on the city streets Christmas Day. He guessed many of them might have been tourists.

Tasha whistled against the cold and the snowflakes that waltzed with the wind. The light, trendy red coat she'd grabbed apparently wasn't warm enough.

He took off his scarf and put it around her neck.

"Zed, you'll freeze!"

He grit his teeth against the cold. As much as he was uncomfortable, there was something about Tasha that made him happy to take care of her. "I'll be fine."

"Well, at least let's take the free shuttle to get us there quicker," she said.

He nodded.

They scurried to the corner to catch the next shuttle. By the time they arrived at Union Station, the old feelings of anxiety started to return. While his initial visit to Union Station with Tasha on her birthday was hard, it was just the tip of the iceberg. Now his deeper fears and hurts were bubbling to the surface. Tasha grabbed his hand and squeezed it as if she sensed his apprehension.

Her kind gesture touched him. "Man, as a kid, I had a love-hate relationship with this place."

He guided them toward the entrance and held open the door for her.

They went inside and she followed him to one of the high vintage booths. He sat, and a huge breath whooshed out of him. "A part of me hates how my dad changed this place for me." Zed paused. His eyes roamed the vast structure. "He made me loathe it."

He took a moment to do a little people watching before he continued. "He was the happiest I ever saw him when leaving to go away on business—I mean, like sublime pleasure for real. He never looked at my mother or me that way. It's been hard to come here. For me, it's a harsh reminder of abandonment, rejection and being second choice. When I see all the happy families at the holidays, something I never had, it hurts. Nevertheless, there's a part of me that wants to love the place and everything it stands for at Christmas—love, joy. As a little kid, I wondered what was wrong with me. Why was I so unlovable that Dad couldn't feel about me the way he felt about his job?"

"Oh, Zed. I'm so sorry."

"Not as sorry as I am."

"Have you forgiven him?"

His lips formed a rigid line. "You figure he deserves that?" he said coolly.

"He doesn't," she replied.

Her answer caught him off guard.

"None of us do. But that's what Christmas is about. The beauty of God's forgiving heart toward us."

"Tasha, I decided to come here today to take back my life, to take back the joy of the holidays he stole from me." He let out a hard breath. "Oh, man. I'm sorry for being such a downer. And on Christmas, too."

Tasha shook her head in protest. "You spoke your truth. You needed to vent. And that's what friends are for. To listen and sometimes just be there."

He pulled her up and gave her a friendly hug. "Thank you."

She gently patted his back. When she pulled away, he readied himself for a confession. "Believe it or not, this trip wasn't just about me."

Tasha looked confused.

"I remember how you said your holiday breakups made you feel—unappreciated and less than."

"Thanks for the reminder. I thought you didn't want to be a downer."

"I've got a surprise for you," he announced. "Wait here." He sprinted to the Hotel Crawford front desk, which was inside Union Station. A customer service agent from behind the desk handed him a decorative shopping sack. He headed back her way.

"Close your eyes," he ordered.

"Why?"

"Were you a difficult child, too?" he teased.

"Okay." She closed her eyes.

He removed a tiara from the sack and placed it on her head.

"What in the world?" She reached up and felt around her head. Her eyes flew open.

Next, he removed a bouquet of roses from the bag.

"Zed!" Tasha cried.

He handed the flowers to her and held his arm out for her to take.

"I feel like Miss America." She rapidly looked around. "Is there a runway somewhere? I'm warning you. I won't participate in the swimsuit competition. I'm against it, on principle." He heard the teasing in her voice.

"Did you ever consider a career as a stand-up comedian?" he asked.

She blushed. "No, not really."

"Good thing," he quipped. "Now, enough with the jokes. Just follow me."

He led her toward the exit.

"But we just got here," she cried.

"Trust me."

Once outside, he guided her to a horse-drawn carriage in front of the building. The carriage, driver and horses were dressed festively. The impressive equines were white as winter snow.

She gazed at him, her eyes sparkling with wonder. "What's going on?"

He just grinned as he led her to the carriage and nodded toward the driver. Zed extended his hand to her. "My lady."

After helping her into the high seat, he joined her. There was a thick plaid blanket on the seat. Zed placed it around their legs.

"Just one moment, sir," he said to the driver. He quickly texted on his phone.

One of the horses neighed. Both animals shuffled and shimmied as the driver spoke softly to them.

After a minute or so, a young woman wearing an apron exited the station and walked their way. She held two paper cups.

"Can't have Christmas without hot chocolate," he announced.

The girl handed them the steaming cups, and he gave her a hefty tip. "Thanks."

"We're ready now," he told the driver. The driver made a clucking sound with his tongue and jostled the reins. The horses began to slowly move.

Zed noticed passersby observing Tasha with interest.

"Zed, although I appreciate the thought, I feel a little silly wearing this tiara."

He turned her way. "That may just be the point."

"How so?" she asked.

"Maybe you've been a little uncomfortable celebrating yourself, like God and others do. You're kind with a big heart. You help so many others and make them feel special. Today's your day."

"I've never liked attention," she said.

"Nevertheless, you didn't deserve to be dismissed and made to feel invisible by those guys who broke up with you during the holidays."

His gaze connected with hers. "They were idiots. They discarded a rare treasure—a princess."

"A princess? Really? Don't you think that's a bit of a stretch?"

"No. Consider this. God calls Himself the greatest King. You're His daughter. That makes you a princess."

She broke eye contact with him. "In my past I never felt that way. Whenever I was vulnerable with guys before, I always found myself crushed like a delicate flower under a boot." Her gaze reconnected with his. "Thanks for making this Christmas so special. It's one of the best I've had. Ever. You've set the bar high. I just wish I could do something for you today. To make it special for you, too."

"You already have," he said.

She looked puzzled. "How?"

"By being here with me." She'd helped ease the anxiety and sadness he felt about the place. And the memory they'd made today would be something he could revisit in his mind whenever he wished, which would further lessen the impact of his painful past.

After the carriage ride, on the way home, they picked up a holiday meal from the grocery store. When they got back to the Victorian, Zed made a fire and Tasha suggested they eat in front of the fireplace—an idea he liked. He found a large card table in one of the closets and added a festive tablecloth to it.

As they ate, an unusual sense of peace overtook him. Was this what healthy relationships felt like? The thought made him both curious and afraid.

His mother had told him stories of how his dad had wooed her before they were married. She'd left her home in Tennessee and everything she knew to move across the country to be with him. That was what had made the shock of his ultimate treatment and disregard hurt so much. She'd opened her heart and been vulnerable and she'd been discarded like a wrapper after a fast-food meal.

Zed had not only vowed to never be like his father, in the man's cruel treatment of his family, but he'd also promised himself he wouldn't be like his mother, who gave the power to define who she was to someone else.

While Tasha was sweet and an amazing lady, he couldn't let her get to him. He'd learned, first-hand, the cost of vulnerability. And the price was too high.

Chapter Eight

The emotional high of Christmas was quickly overshadowed for Tasha when, three days after the holiday, she headed to church with her new husband for the first time. She'd not only have to face the congregation, but more important, Pastor Landry, too.

She wished they could have gone to Zed's church instead. But they decided for their brief marriage to go to her church since she was on staff there and her absence would be harder to navigate.

As Zed pulled into the church lot and parked, Tasha asked if they could sit for a moment because she needed to gather her courage. She nervously tapped her Bible that rested in her lap. Outside, patches of damp winter brown grass peeked out from the places where Colorado sun had melted the snow.

"You all right?" Zed said.

She shook her head. "In theory, our plan to save your house sounded good. And it is, for the reasons we're doing it. But I must confess, we did this all so fast, there are consequences I didn't consider."

Zed cocked his head. "Like what?"

"Well, for one, my church strongly urges counseling before marriage. It's mandatory for people who wish to get married at the church. And here I am, the singles' pastor and wedding planner, no less, who basically eloped, shotgun style—blowing that rule to smithereens."

Compassion filled his eyes. His large right hand covered her left hand. "I'm sorry. I'm to blame for putting you in this situation."

"No, you didn't force me. I went along willingly."

"Nevertheless, I didn't mean to complicate your life." He stared out at the winter scene in front of them. "Know this, Tasha. No matter the reasons why we did this, for these three months, in every way honorable, I'm your husband. I'll stand with you, support you. And I've got you."

She avoided his penetrating stare. Tasha didn't want him to see how his words had impacted her. She'd never had a man in her life who so fiercely cared about her well-being.

Zed squeezed her hand. "Tasha, I got you," he repeated in a softer, gentler tone.

She nodded. "Let's go in."

After opening his door, Zed climbed out and jaunted around to hers. The first time Zed had done this, her urge had been to open the door herself. *I'm a strong, independent woman, not some helpless waif.* But she'd suddenly remembered something she'd read in a book called *God's Daughters.* It said, "God thought his daughters should be pampered and seen like the royalty they were in the Lord's eyes." Now she was so used to Zed's gentlemanly gesture, she just waited for it.

When Zed opened her door, she accepted his outstretched hand. He steadied her and helped her avoid a menacing puddle next to the vehicle.

They followed the groups of people who streamed from the parking lot into the church. Tasha noticed a few curious stares as Zed walked beside her, and her heart sped up when she saw Pastor Landry standing at the door, greeting people.

Zed took her hand, as if sensing her anxiety. "We got this."

As they reached the front door, the pastor's eyes sparkled with warmth, which shifted to mild curiosity when he saw Zed.

"Tasha, good to see you. How was your Christmas holiday?"

Her breath hitched. "Eventful," she said. *Might as well dive in.*

"Is that right?" the pastor said in a friendly tone that wasn't overly inquisitive. A clue he had no idea how meaningful her one-word declaration was. Yet.

"Pastor Landry, this is Zed."

Pastor Landry grinned wide and enthusiastically pumped Zed's hand. "We're glad to have you join us today."

"Thank you," Zed replied.

"We love us some Tasha here," the pastor declared.

Zed turned to her. "I so get that," he said.

The first flame of real curiosity flickered in the pastor's eyes.

Her heart raced. She licked her lips. Best to just get it over with. "Pastor Landry, I'd like you to meet my husband."

Pastor Landry's pale cheeks rapidly flushed a deep red. His eyes danced between Zed and her.

She tried to smile, but the corners of her mouth felt like they had weights attached to them. "Surprise, I got married!" Hearing the unintended tremor in her voice, due to her nerves, she flashed her ring for proof.

Tasha knew Pastor Landry's expressions well enough to discern the wheels rapidly churning in his brain. However, the pastor was an expert at keeping a calm exterior—a trick of his trade.

"Well, I guess congratulations are in order." As he gave her a friendly side hug, she could feel a slight stiffness in his body. He shook Zed's hand again, as if he didn't know what else to do.

"Welcome to our family, Zed. Enjoy the service," he said.

A line was developing behind her to greet the pastor, so she let Zed gently guide her into the church foyer. The sanctuary was still adorned in the bright decorations of Christmas. "See, that wasn't so bad," Zed declared.

Tasha wasn't so sure, but she gave him a reassuring smile. She decided she'd enjoy the service rather than fretting.

When services started, Tasha sang the Christmas hymns enthusiastically. She marveled at the man standing next to her. She'd always been alone. It was hard to believe she had a partner— even if he was as temporary as a fake tattoo.

After church, the pastor kindly wished them well before they exited the sanctuary. When Tasha got in the car, relief washed over her. Maybe Zed was right that everything would be fine.

Zed fired up the engine. As he started to drive away, her phone pinged and she retrieved it from her purse. It was a text from Pastor Landry.

We need to talk. Set up a meeting with my assistant.

Tasha's optimism whooshed out of her. The troubling text bothered her all the way home.

When they got to the house, her eyes went to the Christmas tree as soon as she stepped inside. It looked even more enchanting with daylight bathing the sparkling ornaments in light.

"Why can't it be Christmas every day?" she asked as Zed helped her off with her coat.

"When you said that, I could suddenly see you as a small, expectant little girl standing with your mother in front of this house—all wistful and hopeful, with childlike faith in Christmas."

"Yeah?" She'd tried to hide her mood change since the text, but her optimism was waning.

"Hey, what's wrong?" Zed asked.

Her eyes remained on the tree. She bit her lip to stop it from trembling. "I got a text from Pastor Landry. He wants to meet with me."

"Is it about me?"

"I'm guessing so." She rubbed her neck to remove a stubborn kink.

"I'll go with you," he replied.

She was surprised by the fierce protectiveness she heard in his voice. However, she shook her head in protest. "I don't think that's a good idea." She went to the kitchen and removed a plastic container of leftover turkey from the fridge. Opening it, she took a few slices and offered some to him.

"Thanks." It amazed her how they seemed to already be syncing. She'd naturally thought of him when she got herself something to eat. He took a sliver of cold turkey she offered him.

"It's not that I don't appreciate your offer. I do. But I know the church's terrain a little better than you. And I don't want to tangle you up in my problems. I got this." She hoped that was true.

When Tasha refused his help with her pastor, Zed saw the same determination on her face that had been there the first time they met and she'd declared marriage wasn't the endgame for every woman. His heart stirred with admiration.

How he wished his mother had had such inner strength. Instead, she'd defined who she was and her worth by his father's yardstick. When his dad chose his work over her and his home, it was as if she had no identity, as if she was invisible. How different would her life have been if she'd had belief in herself, independent of his dad's definition of her?

He looked around his childhood home. With the combination of some of his furniture and Tasha's belongings, the old Victorian had gained new life and warmth. Like a real home. But this wasn't a real home. His definition of home, for himself, was his career. And he wouldn't hurt someone as sweet as Tasha, or any other woman, by giving only a part of himself, as his dad had done. He'd seen how it had destroyed his mother and wouldn't be able to forgive himself if he crushed Tasha's independent spirit.

He headed upstairs to change out of his church clothes. When he returned downstairs, he heard a squealing teapot, which had obviously reached its peak boil. Tasha was staring out the kitchen window.

He removed the teapot from the fire. "What's up?" he asked. "I think the teapot might have been heard squealing in the next county."

"Sorry," she replied. "When it rains, it pours. We've got a new wrinkle to iron out. I just got a text from the singles' group. They want to meet with us. I'm sorry to have to put you through this," Tasha said. "They want to have some sort of gathering for us before the New Year."

"You're helping me save my house. I owe you, big time. I'm happy to meet with them."

And that was how a couple days later they found themselves, yet again, at Tasha's church. Zed sensed Tasha's apprehension. "Tash, it's fine. While I'm not a fan of the spotlight, I'll do it for you," Zed said. "Actually, I'm surprised so many of them are around just after Christmas."

"Normally, they wouldn't be. But a bunch of them signed up to go on a mission trip to Mexico just after the New Year. They decided to celebrate Thanksgiving with their families and to stay here for the Christmas holiday, since it was so close to the mission trip date.

"Just so you know, we'll be flying solo in there. It's a Q and A, so they could ask anything. It could get unpredictable."

"Kinda like this whole marriage thing?" he said.

Tasha laughed. "Yeah, you're right. We're becoming experts at uncharted waters, I guess. I just want to be as authentic as possible, without revealing our arrangement."

As they neared the front door, a young woman burst through it. Her bright grin lit up her heart-shaped face.

"That's Calista Gregory. She's a member of the singles' group and a mentee of mine. She's a hopeless romantic."

The girl rushed toward Tasha and hugged her. After they disengaged, she gave Zed a shy glance. "I couldn't wait to meet you," she said to him. She swiped her dark micro-braids out of her face. "I'm Calista Gregory."

"Hi, Calista. I'm Zed. Tasha speaks very fondly of you."

Calista's light-skinned complexion flushed. "Me? Really?"

"Yes," he replied.

"I'm flattered." The girl's phone pinged and she glanced at it. "Could you guys give us just a few more minutes?"

"Sure," Tasha said.

"Okay. I've got to get back inside. I'll text you when we're ready." Calista sprinted back to the front door and disappeared into the church.

While they waited, Tasha told him that Calista was one of her favorite singles. "In a lot of ways, she reminds me of myself when I was her age. She's a hopeless romantic and she's obsessed with marriage."

Zed considered Tasha's remark. What had happened to make Tasha do a one-eighty turn in her view of marriage? Had the holiday break-ups shattered her heart until it was beyond repair? If that was the case, it made him sad. She was a sweet lady. If anybody understood a heart finally bruised beyond repair, he did. He'd seen his mother live it out.

"My prayer for Calista is that she'll have a more balanced view of marriage," Tasha said. "There's nothing wrong with desiring it. However, I think she puts it on an unrealistic pedestal, like it's the answer to everything, even over her relationship with the Lord."

Tasha's phone chimed and she looked at the screen. "They're ready for us."

When they went inside, Tasha led him to the church's fellowship hall, which was packed. Pink and red crepe paper streamers, along with red, white and pink balloons covered the hall. A table was set up with red velvet cupcakes and a three-tiered white cake adorned with ruby-red rose blossoms.

Tasha shot him a concerned glance. He returned it with a silent look of assurance that everything would be fine.

Calista approached them. "Since you didn't have a traditional wedding and reception, we thought we'd throw a little something-something for you." The girl's dark eyes eagerly watched them, as if looking for a happy response.

Apprehension tightened Zed's chest. He took pride in being authentic. To navigate the meeting with Calista and others would be a wieldy ride, as he attempted to be honorable but not expose their fake relationship. This would be the real test; one he hoped they could pass.

Tasha's eyes teared up at the singles' group's gesture. Which was perfect for the moment. She knew Calista would think she was touched. And she truly was. But it also made things harder for her, knowing her and Zed's real arrangement.

"Awww, baby," Zed said.

Tasha's eyes connected with his. Something felt wrong about him putting on an act. However, she was shocked to find sincerity pouring from his eyes. He took out a handkerchief from his breast pocket and gently wiped her tears away.

Calista clutched her chest with both hands, as if she was overwhelmed by Zed's gesture. "Tasha, see there, that's just the kind of man I want."

Just wait. He'll be available in a few months. Her humorous thought felt bittersweet as she watched her temporary husband return his handkerchief to his pocket.

Calista led them to a podium with two chairs, also decorated with streamers and balloons, then spoke into the mic. "The lovebirds are here, y'all."

Thunderous applause arose from the audience. Several "woo-hoos" rang out, as well as a few friendly catcalls. People started jumping up like popcorn, until they had a standing ovation, as well.

Zed grabbed her hand. His rapid heartbeat pulsed through his fingers, and she gently squeezed his hand in silent encouragement.

The audience's celebration went on for a few minutes before Calista gestured for them to sit. "Thanks, everybody. We've got a lot to cover tonight and even a few surprises for the newlyweds." She turned and winked their way.

Tasha attempted to keep the contented smile on her face. Inside, nerves twisted her stomach at Calista's announcement.

Calista picked up a stack of cue cards. "Let's get started. We'd like to get through as many of your questions as possible. First question—your romance was a whirlwind, to say the least. What was it about each other that was different, that you just knew so quickly you were the ones for each other?"

Tasha rapidly tried to compose an answer in her mind.

"Let's start with you, Zed. We all know why we love us some Miss Tasha. Do share why you do?"

There was uproarious applause again.

"What was it about her that just did it for you?" Calista continued.

Zed's eyes bored into Tasha's, like he was searching their depths for something. "Well, although it's hard to put into words, I'll try. Because you guys know and love her, I think you kind of get it. I mean, really, how can anyone that knows her not love her?"

There was more applause.

While Zed's answer should have touched her heart, instead, an emotional dart penetrated it at his statement. Memories of the many guys she'd loved and given her heart to, who'd dumped her as easily as yesterday's news, made Zed's statement questionable. Everybody she'd known hadn't felt that way, especially the ones she'd so desperately wanted to love her.

When the applause died down, silence blanketed the place. The group was eagerly waiting for Zed's next words. Fidgeting with the mic, he glanced around. He looked her way, but she couldn't read the emotions in his eyes.

"I guess the best way to say it is, when I met Tasha, it was like I came home."

Her heart lurched. He was good. And he was truthful. He had come home—to *his* home.

He continued. "Home, in a sense of that place that's your haven, your refuge, that contains the most precious things to you. Where you feel, no matter what, you're protected and loved."

His voice trembled slightly at his last few words. Whether his words were true or not, she instinctively knew he was touched by something. Maybe he'd conjured up images of his mother and their love for each other. Kind of like when actors used real-life experiences to help them bring emotion to a scene.

Several women audibly sighed in the audience, and there was another round of applause.

"That's beautiful. And so romantic. Thanks for sharing," Calista said. She took the mic from him and approached Tasha. "And what about you,

Tasha? What was it about Zed that rocked your world?"

Laughter erupted in the audience.

She took the mic from Calista. "Well, I guess, playing off of Zed's words about feeling he'd found his home…" She turned to him. "For me, it was the first time in my life that I wanted to open the door fully to my heart. It's not that I hadn't fallen for guys before—after all, you guys lived with me through my dating journey."

"Yeah, we did," Calista said. "And some of us are still going through therapy over it."

The audience roared with laughter.

"But before Zed, I'd never met someone I could just be myself around without fear." She realized that the words she spoke were true.

Calista sighed. "Wow, I don't know about y'all but I think I'm a little jealous right now. Well, keeping it real, I'm a lot jelly." She flipped to another of the cue cards she was holding. "Next question… Some people say you should trust God and wait on Him to bring your mate. Others say you must be proactive, using dating sites, stuff like that. What was you guys' experience?"

Clueless how to respond, Tasha was grateful when Zed took the mic. "I got this one. To be honest, I don't think there's a black-and-white answer to that. God can move in amazing ways. I think a person's foundation should always be to trust the Lord. But be open to God using circumstances to lead and guide. For Tash and me, I think the Lord used serendipity for our paths to cross."

Pride filled Tasha at Zed's wise answer. And he'd even stayed true to how they really met. She gazed at the enrapt audience. Pride gave way to guilt. They were hanging on every word. The group saw her and Zed as examples of God orchestrating a love story. *Oh, Lord, I'm sorry.*

Zed returned to his seat next to her, taking her hand as if he'd read her mind. Whether he had or not, she wasn't sure. But the gesture helped her get through the battery of other questions that came their way until, mercifully, the Q and A finally ended.

"Hey, guys, can we thank Tasha and Zed for sharing?"

The audience clapped, then they received a standing ovation. Once Calista finally settled the group back down, she produced a Cheshire-cat grin. "So we have a little surprise for the newlyweds."

Tasha gave Zed a curious look before providing the same to Calista.

"As we said, since we weren't able to participate in your ceremony, we thought we'd recreate it here for you."

A group of musicians entered the room, carrying their instruments to the stage. And then Pastor Landry appeared.

"What's going on?" Tasha mouthed to Calista.

"Since you never knew your dad, and Pastor Landry is like a spiritual father to you, we thought you could have your father-daughter dance with him," Calista said.

Tasha clutched her chest, truly touched at their thoughtfulness. Even so, she wanted to escape the room, as well as from her and Zed's charade.

Pastor Landry reached out his hand to her. The musicians began to play "Ribbon in the Sky," a favorite of hers. Not able to escape, Tasha stood and took Pastor Landry's hand.

The stage lights turned a soft pink, with a spotlight shining on the pair. Calista gently led Zed from the stage.

Pastor Landry looked at her with a mixture of love and pride. Tasha's heart turned within her. If only she'd had a real father who had felt the same way. She soaked up the pastor's honest affection for her.

As they started to waltz, Pastor Landry caught her eye. He spoke softly, only for her ears. "Tasha, since we're here now, let's discuss what I wanted to talk to you about when I texted you. You skipped protocol. As a leader, you set an example for others. We don't want your actions to set a precedent."

Tasha nodded. "I'm sorry. Everything happened so fast." She told him the truth, about their three-month marriage agreement.

Pastor Landry seemed momentarily stumped. His surprised expression finally gave way to a serious one, with a hint of kindness. "While you skipped protocol, and entered this most unusual agreement, I'd encourage you, now that you're married, to open your heart, regardless of the three-month thing. Maybe this could be more— maybe the door was opened to force you to deal with your heart and disappointments."

Tasha tried to speak, but emotion choked out her voice. She'd been down the road of repeatedly opening her heart, only to have it stomped on and left for dead. She wasn't interested in an instant replay. Ever.

The song finally ended. Pastor Landry kissed her forehead, like a real father would have done. Then he bowed and left the stage. Tasha started to follow him, but Calista stopped her.

"Not so fast. We've got a special song for the bride and groom's first dance," she said. She nodded toward the musicians. As the song began, Tasha recognized her favorite love song, "Because You Loved Me." In the past, she'd repeatedly said she'd have the song at her wedding—when she had still believed in and hoped for love.

"Zed, please join your lovely bride."

Zed approached Tasha. With one hand he clasped hers, and his other went around her waist.

Tasha gazed into his beautiful eyes as she fought her mixed feelings. Since childhood she'd dreamed of a moment such as this—her first dance with her husband. And ironically, now she had it, but she really didn't because of their relationship facade. Tears stung her eyes and dripped down her cheek.

Irrational anger filled her. While she should have applauded his amazing acting, it only upset her more. She didn't deserve this—to always live in a fantasy world, without real fulfillment as she had once wanted. Now she just wanted to be done with this arrangement and get on with her life. Zed was like the proverbial carrot, cruelly dangled in front of her, never to be captured.

She couldn't wait to really start her life—after their three-month fiasco was finally over. Then she could finally supplement her wedding planning by adding the wedding venue business to it.

She was fine on her own. She'd learned to love herself and found the greatest love story of all in her relationship with the Lord. She needed nothing else. *Yes, sirree, I'm more than fine alone.*

She wiped her wet cheeks and held her head high. Feeling new resolve, she decided she'd prove to herself that Zed wasn't all that and she still had control of herself when it came to him. She gave him a serious smooch. There. She'd done it. And she felt nothing. Nada. Zilch. Zero.

It was only when she came to, splayed across the stage, that she realized she'd fainted.

Zed hovered over his wife as she lay crumpled on the church recreation hall center stage floor. Her eyes fluttered rapidly, like an overworked moth. Her gaze finally fixed on him.

"Tash, are you all right?"

Tasha licked her lips. Her scrutiny went past him to the others surrounding her, including the pastor and Calista.

Tasha tried to sit up. "I'm fine. I didn't eat much today. Sometimes I have trouble with low blood sugar."

Zed gripped her upper body and slowly pulled her up. Thankfully, he'd caught her before she'd hit the ground. He'd been able to gently lay her on the floor.

"Calista, why don't you get Tasha some water," Pastor Landry said. "And maybe a piece of the cake we made for them, to help with her blood sugar."

"I'm on it," Calista declared stoically, as if she'd been given orders by a drill sergeant.

Zed drew Tasha to himself, as an anchor to

steady her. He didn't care whether she liked it or not. She needed him. Period.

To his surprise, she gently laid her head on his shoulder, obviously grateful for his support.

Pastor Landry went to the podium to address the concerned crowd. People's voices carried like an overactive beehive.

"Folks, everything is all right. Tasha is going to be fine. We'll give her a moment to get her bearings and then we'll let the newlyweds cut their cake."

Zed led Tasha to her seat on stage and sat beside her. Her brown curls, pressed against his face, smelled faintly of jasmine. He imperceptibly moved his nose a little closer, to take in the wonderful scent of her.

His heart was dancing hard. In the commotion with Tasha, he'd ignored the way his chest thrummed, but now...

It had started at that kiss. He'd been startled by Tasha's gesture. Something real had happened during the embrace.

He felt a smile teasing his lips. Had Tasha really fainted because of lack of food? Or had she been as blown out of the water as he had by that kiss?

Tasha chose that moment to raise her head. Apparently noticing something in his expression, she sat back and disengaged from him.

"What?" she asked.

Zed tried to play it off. It would serve no good whatsoever to talk about it. For either of them. "Nothing. I'm just happy you're going to be all right."

Her stare remained locked on him until her eyes finally lit up, as if she'd become aware of something. "Oh, wow! You're gloating."

He stared at her, amazed. No woman had ever been able to read him so well. Not since his mother. He searched in vain for an explanation, without success.

"You think I fainted because your kiss was all that and a bag of chips." She shook her head in apparent wonder. "You might as well strut and preen across the stage like a proud peacock."

"Tasha—" he protested.

A small grin flirted on her lips, as well. "Don't deny it. Your man card just got an upgrade, right?"

He chuckled hard. "Well, your reaction confirms I've got skills."

Astonishment rolled across her face.

"I'm just saying." He'd admitted the truth. He figured he might as well have some fun with it, to get her goat.

She sat back, pressing her spine hard against the back of the chair. Her lips twitched as if she was fighting the grin on her face. "Well, I'll have you know it's true that I sometimes have low blood sugar when I don't eat."

He raised his hands in surrender. "There's more than one kind of sugar that when it goes missing too long it can make a lady weak."

Tasha gave him an incredulous look. "Really? Just, really?" Then the laughter she'd held at bay escaped in billows of joy.

Chapter Nine

Just before the New Year, Tasha remembered Zed's odd gift of the shoebox and Aunt Zora's letter. She retrieved the shoebox just before bed, then crawled under the smooth-as-butter bedcovers, enjoying the gentle whir of the steam heat coming from the registers.

She untied the ribbon and opened the box. Inside, besides the letter, were a few shiny marbles, some baseball cards smudged and faded with age and a photo of what appeared to be Zed as a boy. Wearing a sky blue little suit and matching cap, he stood, smiling brightly, in front of a train caboose. Finally, there was a black-and-white photo of a beautiful woman. Tasha guessed it was Zed's mother. She had the same light eyes and matching dimples. Although she was smiling, the grin didn't reach her eyes, which were lovely, but infinitely sad.

Tasha slowly unfurled Aunt Zora's letter and began to read.

To my beloved Zed's wife,

You must be curious about receiving a letter from a stranger. My apologies. I assume you've heard of me from Zed and my lovely will. You probably think I was a little eccentric. Oh, sweetie. I was a lot eccentric. I wear the title proudly.

In an odd way, I feel like I know you. I'm sure that makes no sense to you. But I believe prayer knows no bounds and can transcend time and worlds. And believe me when I tell you, I prayed on my old arthritic knees many a night for you, hoping the Lord would handpick you to bring into Zed's life. Even if I had to force my nephew's hand a bit to make it happen.

While I've done all I can to throw you together, I can't manufacture love. I can only hope I've made the atmosphere ripe for the possibility of it, if it's not there. But I also realize God gave man free will. Even if Zed walks away after three months, at least he'll have no regrets in old age that he didn't give marriage a try.

Zed is a good man. He's a little rough and

tattered around the emotional edges, due to some hurts and disappointments—but like they say about a house, he's got good bones. Per my lovely will, I know you two are together for at least three months.

If you consider Zedrick Grant Evans like a really good book or meal that you want to savor, and get to know him, you will discover treasure. Despite my best-laid plans, I know you don't have to take my advice. But I promise, if you do, the journey will be as fulfilling as the destination.

By the way, I realize I've assumed much here—that Zed married without love, to fulfill my wishes. If by some wonderful, amazing twist he met someone and fell in love and is happily married, then I am over the moon happy for you both. I pray this letter will serve to give you greater insight into your husband—a man more precious than gold. And yes, I'm biased.

So, let me get to the point. My dear sister's life was hard. It was painful to see Evelyn suffer in her marriage.

Besides me, she only had Zed to confide in. She ultimately realized she depended on her son, who was just a child, too much for that. Her kid was not meant to bear the weight of her baggage and emotional issues on his young shoulders. It was a role his absentee father should have filled. So Zed might not know the full story.

While Evelyn knew Zed's dad's job was his true mistress, I am sad to say there were rumors that wasn't his only mistress and that he might have reconnected and had a sustained relationship with a childhood sweetheart from Denver.

I never brought this up with my nephew because it was unsubstantiated, but living in a small town, such as Vista Peak, I wouldn't be surprised if Zed got wind of the rumors, too. Whether it was true or not, his mother lived with this possible knowledge, which further added to her burden.

I tell you this, my dear, so you have some context of the things that have hardened our boy's heart to love. In his home, he didn't see an example of true love and how wonderful it can be.

Oh, and if you're wondering about the other items in the box, Zed loved trains because of his dad, and the marbles and baseball cards were handed down from his father. The photo of the lady is his mother.

I kept this box as a reminder of the little boy I knew, who loved his family and longed for a happy home. I pray I've given you some insight into my nephew that will help you understand the man you married.

Sincerely,
Zora

The bottom dropped out of Tasha's stomach. Zed's wounds might have gone far deeper than she'd ever thought.

In her past relationships, she'd always been drawn to broken men, feeling she could save them with her love. Her shattered heart was evidence of how wrong she'd been. In therapy, she'd learned that she might have gravitated toward broken men because subconsciously she didn't feel she deserved better, and the only way she figured she could capture love was by saving a man and earning his adoration.

A troubling question teased the edge of her brain. Subconsciously, did she think she was Zed's life preserver, too?

Aunt Zora's troubling correspondence invaded Tasha's thoughts the next day, the last day of the year. She decided to walk to the town square to Nate's Nest, the town diner.

As she pushed open the door to the diner, the little bell rang, which always made her smile.

She loved this little touch from a bygone era. The place felt like home. She and her mother had been coming here since her childhood visits to Zed's neighborhood to view the Victorians at Christmas.

After he got to know them during their holiday visits, Nate Sr., the diner's founder, who never met a stranger, had often quietly comped her and her mother's meals, aware of her single mother's strained finances. And Tasha had spent many afternoons after her college classes studying at the diner under the watchful eye of Nate Sr. He'd died a few years before her mother. His son, Nate Jr., now ran the place.

"Tasha!" Nate Jr. said warmly. He waved at her from behind the counter, where patrons sat if they didn't want a booth or table.

While Nate had his father's lanky frame, he had his Native American mother's beautiful darker coloring and eyes. His coal-black hair was now accented with more than a few gray hairs. Where did time go?

To her surprise, he wagged his finger at her, and his expression turned stern. "I've got a bone to pick with you, young lady. Why did I have to find out through the grapevine that you married one of Vista Peak's most notorious bachelors?"

Tasha blushed. "I'm sorry."

A slow smile reappeared on Nate's face. "While

I was slightly hurt, I'm mostly pulling your leg. I'm happy for you and Zed."

Nate Jr. scooted from behind the counter and gave her a hardy side hug. "How you doing, otherwise?" His sable-brown eyes looked at her with concern. "I mean really," he said. "I know the holidays can be hard. I still miss my dad, and I'm sure you must miss your mom. She was sweet as honey on sugar."

"I have my moments," she said. "About the marriage thing—it was sort of a whirlwind."

Nate Jr. observed her as if he had more questions but decided against prying. "Well, you're certainly the talk of the town. Everybody wants to know how you accomplished the Herculean task of capturing the elusive Mr. Evans."

She laughed. "That's highly privileged information."

"Well, all I've got to say is that it's about time somebody discovered one of Vista Peak's pearls. Zed Evans is a blessed man."

Nate Jr's words touched her. And made her sad. What would he think when she was divorced in a few months? Why couldn't his words have been true? Why couldn't someone have discovered her like a jewel? Instead, she had a relationship as fake as cubic zirconium.

Tasha's phone pinged, and a glance at it showed a text from a former bridal client.

Nate Jr. looked past her to the small line of people that had gathered up front to pay their bill. "Sweetie, take a seat wherever you'd like. And your meal is on the house. As a belated wedding gift." He headed toward the counter and the waiting patrons.

Tasha found an empty booth near the window as she reviewed her text from Shayla Mitchell-Jons, whose wedding she'd planned the previous year.

Tasha. Hey! Matt and I just celebrated our first year of marriage. I've got news. We're expecting our first child! You were such a part of making our big day wonderful, I wanted to share the news with you and wish you a happy New Year. I hope you are doing good. May all your dreams come true.

"Can I take your order?"

Tasha looked up to find a new waitress she didn't recognize. The girl looked college age and Tasha guessed she probably went to Vista Peak West.

She hadn't had a chance to review the menu, but she knew it by heart. "I'll have the number four special, with sausage links and half orange juice, half cranberry juice, with a dash of sparkling water."

The girl's dark eyebrows wiggled, probably at Tasha's unusual beverage order. She scribbled on her order pad. "Got it. Thanks." The waitress left.

Tasha texted Shayla her congratulations. Her client was living out the life she'd once hoped for herself. She remembered Shayla's effervescent joy as they planned her wedding, as well as her declaration that God gave her the desires of her heart with her amazing fiancé. The comment had unexpectedly sliced through Tasha's heart. The girl was barely out of college, and she'd found love. Yet, Tasha had waited and longed for the same for over thirty-five years, before her heart had finally been shattered beyond repair. And what did she have to show for it? A fake marriage that in some ways mocked her even more. Had she not been worthy of the real thing? Did God favor some people over others?

She shut down the troubling thoughts before they took her down a road she wasn't ready to travel.

Zed loosened his tie as he entered the Victorian. Following an amazing smell to the kitchen, he found a note on the counter from Tasha. "Add a side salad to the main dish—a roast in the slow cooker—then simply insert in mouth and swallow." She'd drawn a little happy face emoji to end the note.

Many nights growing up, he'd come home from school to a dark house. This was a clue that his mother was sequestered in her room, in the throes of depression. He'd had to fend for himself and often lived off peanut butter and jelly sandwiches.

How he'd longed for a house filled with the smells of dinner, a bright, happy place that he was eager to come home to, like Tasha had made the Victorian. Not that he hadn't had happy times with his mother—he had. Unfortunately, the darker, sadder times occurred more often than he'd wished.

Zed halted his thought. This wasn't real. Tasha was a Band-Aid, not the cure for his life. She wasn't interested in a real marriage, and neither was he.

He grabbed a fork and captured a piece of roast along with a carrot from the simmering pot.

"Hey."

Lost in his thoughts, he hadn't realized Tasha had come home.

"Hey, yourself," he said. He felt like a kid caught mid-prank, having been spotted eating from the slow cooker.

She had a mock stern look on her face, softened by her smile. "Seriously, I know your mother taught you better than that."

He grinned sheepishly and pointed a finger to

his brain. "It's all about strategy. I'm saving on dirtying dishes. Less for us to wash." He winked at his own brilliance.

"First, Einstein, we don't wash the dishes. The dishwasher does that. Second, that was truly the most pitiful excuse ever for bad manners."

He chuckled as he popped the food he'd secured into his mouth.

"Seriously, though," Tasha said. "I have a question. Might I use one of the spare rooms upstairs for a makeshift office? I'd like to work on my business plan for the New Year, explore some fresh marketing ideas and prep for some upcoming client projects."

"Sure. Take whatever room you'd like."

"Just so you know, I'm a bit of an aesthetic person. Atmosphere matters and inspires me. I may put up pictures of brides, flowers, stuff like that. It'll be a hard-core estrogen zone for a while."

Zed's brows jumped and settled in surprise. "Duly noted. I'll wear my testosterone hazmat suit if I have to enter."

"Hazmat suit. Wow. Zed, may I ask you another question?"

He grabbed a clean dish towel and placed the fork he'd been using on it. "Sure."

"Did you ever want to be married?"

Her question sobered him. "No."

She groaned. "Wow. I think I have a gift."

"For what?" he asked.

"Finding noncommittal men. I'm better than a heat-seeking missile."

Her words hit him in the chest. "Not every noncommittal man is running from commitment. Some have made a choice to commit to other things. I would think you'd understand, as you yourself aren't interested in marriage, by choice."

Tasha studied him. "It wasn't always that way. Searching for love is kind of like being a warrior in a long battle. You fight hard, steel yourself against every defeat, but slowly, with each lost battle, you lose a little bit of your heart, a little bit of yourself. Until that one final loss tips the scales and changes everything. And just like that, your courage, your hope—it's just gone."

Zed's heart ached at the defeat and sadness in Tasha's eyes. He wanted to say something to make her feel better. But he had nothing. In a strange way, he understood her analogy from a different perspective. For many years he'd longed for his dad to come to his senses and realize what a wonderful wife he had and to change the paradigm of his life, putting work in the right perspective. Zed hoped his father would come home one day, admit his mistake and give Zed's mother the love and adoration she desired and deserved. But it never happened. And Zed remembered the day that he, like Tasha, lost hope things would ever change.

"I'm going to head upstairs and take a look at the small bedroom at the end of the hall for my office," she said.

"Do you mind if I come along?" Although he didn't know what to say, he wanted to be with her, to offer her any small comfort he could.

"Sure."

Zed waited in the small corner bedroom while Tasha changed out of her work clothes. The room was just across from his bedroom. It was intimate and cozy, and it would be perfect for a makeshift office for her. It had a feminine feel about it, too, with its cream-corn-yellow wallpaper with tiny, green-leafed daisies. There was a small daybed, a bookshelf and two matching floor lamps. A big, circular Persian rug filled up the space. In the corner, there was a miniature rolltop desk.

When Tasha entered the room, carrying a laptop, she surveyed the space before going to the small closet door in the room and opening it. She pulled out a few boxes, some folded old clothes and a moderate-size bulletin board.

"This bulletin board will be perfect for my vision board for the bride."

"Vision board?" he asked.

"Yes. For every client, I make a personal vision board for the couple. It's mostly to provide a broad overview of the project and a placeholder for notes and reminders, as well as to keep me inspired. Sometimes when things become tedious or challenging, I need to be reminded why I'm doing what I'm doing—that I'm helping facilitate one of the most important days in a couple's lives—a beautiful day that celebrates their love."

Zed wondered if she knew how her face and features lit up when she talked about what she loved. Had it been hard helping others get married, while her constant companion was rejection and unrequited love?

He was surprised to find a lump in his throat. Tasha hadn't deserved what happened to her, just like his mother hadn't deserved her treatment. There was a scripture in the Bible where God talked about wanting to take His children under His wing, so if anything tried to get to them, it would have to get past God first.

He had the urge to cover Tasha from all the hurt and harm she'd experienced. But reality checked his noble thoughts at the door. He was in no place to protect her or any other woman. He'd made his vow and he was a man who kept his word. He knew where his priorities lay. Maybe he was the appetizer before the real meal in Tasha's life. Though her heart was closed, maybe God had a surprise up His sleeve that would blow her mind—a love she never expected.

Yes, he liked that idea. He squished the surprising sadness that bubbled in his chest.

Tasha sat at the small desk in the room and fired up her laptop. "I'd like to show you something," she said. She maneuvered to her email and to an online video.

"Today I got a text from a former client named Shayla, who's celebrating her first year of marriage and expecting a baby. Before they were married, she sent me this video. It's one of my favorites. Unknown to the bride, the groom planned a scavenger hunt, based on the locations of their first dates. In each place, he paid someone to secretly shoot footage of them. When they arrived at the final place, he proposed, and their best friends turned out to be secretly filming the whole thing, and afterward came out from their hiding places, along with family members. I love how the proposal is simple and sweet and how the groom-to-be looks at his fiancée as if she's cherished and priceless."

Zed thought of his impromptu proposal, more like a business pitch, at Union Station, and their subsequent wedding in the cool, sterile halls of the justice of the peace. He felt bad.

Life had certainly taken Tasha down a different path than her client. The woman's sweet proposal surrounded by her J.Crew-dressed friends with perfect hair, smiles and teeth, looked like a commercial for young love in a perfect world.

He studied his grandmother's ring gleaming on Tasha's finger. It glittered from the outdoor light sifting through the lace curtains. It was a beautiful ring, stunning, really. He was sure his grandmother never meant for her wedding ring to be a prop for a loveless relationship. Her own eternal love and tragic loss that the ring had represented until now had been too precious for that.

Chapter Ten

Tasha couldn't wipe the grin off her face. It was New Year's Day, which always brought her a sense of renewed hope and possibility. She felt revived and excited. She found Zed in the kitchen, drinking a glass of orange juice. Milo was thirstily gulping milk from a nearby bowl.

"Zed, what do you think about christening the New Year by going to Nate's Nest? We can share our dreams for the New Year."

"Well, I had some plans in mind, but this is all about you, so your wish for the day is my command."

They dressed and headed to the town square. They decided to walk, due to the unseasonably warm Colorado morning.

Tasha never got tired of strolling through the beautiful historic neighborhood and admiring the homes. When they arrived in the town square, it was obvious that other folks had the same idea of taking advantage of the beautiful day. The square was bustling with clumps of folks going into restaurants and shops, and some sitting in the gazebo in the park square across from the courthouse.

When they arrived at Nate's Nest, Tasha would have thought the President of the United States had entered the place, from Nate's response. He leaped from behind the counter and gave both of them a hug. Afterward, he profusely shook Zed's hand. "You are a man blessed beyond measure— I hope you know that," Nate declared.

Zed looked her way. "I do," he answered.

Her heart started off on a sprint. She took deep breaths. *Slow your roll, girl. He's speaking because he's under contract. Nothing more.*

"Only the best booth in the house for my friends," Nate said. He motioned a waitress over to clean a booth located in a prime spot for viewing the town square. The young girl who'd assisted her when she was at Nate's earlier in the week quickly removed the dirty dishes, glasses and silverware. She then ran a soapy wet rag over the table multiple times.

Nate stretched out a hand, guiding them to the booth, where they both sat.

"By the way, man, I was sorry to hear about your aunt Zora's death. If she was half as sweet as your mother, I'm sure she was a wonderful woman," Nate said.

"Thanks, man. That means a lot," Zed replied.

They both reviewed the menu and relayed their meal choices to the waitress. When the waitress left, Zed observed her.

"So tell me some of your New Year's goals."

She informed Zed that she'd started scouting out possible sites for her wedding venue.

"What about you? What are some of your goals?" she asked.

Zed shared how in addition to saving the Victorian, he wanted to start the year fresh and put the wounds of his father's actions behind him.

"Well, color me shallow. My goal feels pretty silly compared to yours."

Zed shook his head in disagreement. "That's not true. They're yours and they are important to you. That's all that matters."

A random thought crossed her mind. If Zed dealt with the wounds of his father, could that impact his decision to never marry? Tasha shooshed the thought away. It was what she did with guys. She put on rose-tinted glasses and hoped for change, and it always led to the same conclusion—disappointment.

Later, when they arrived home, she peeled off her coat. Before she could even think about it,

Zed had taken it from her and hung it on the coat rack by the stairwell.

"Thanks," she said. *It's amazing how quickly we've become this well-oiled machine.*

Her phone chimed. An unknown number gleamed on the screen, but Tasha recognized it. This was the third time the person had called in a week. They never left a message, but she recognized the Denver area code. She wondered if it was yet another one of the credit companies calling. They were relentless.

She tapped to answer. "Hello."

There was silence on the other end. Was this a crank call?

"Hel-lo," she repeated.

"Is this Violet-Sage Jenkins's daughter?"

Tasha fought her irritation. She hated when strangers called and rudely launched into interrogation.

"Yes. Who's calling, please?"

The man on the other end wheezed and coughed. "My name is Vincent. I knew your mother."

Tasha breathed deeply and tried to maintain her cool.

"I was sorry to hear about her death."

An electric volt pierced Tasha's heart. "Thank you."

"She was a good woman."

Zed appeared from the kitchen with a coffee cup and started to speak but paused when he saw her on the phone. He whispered, "Coffee?"

She gave him a thumbs-up before returning her attention to the call. "Were you a friend of hers?" Tasha wasn't ready to reveal much about herself to the stranger yet.

The man half hiccuped and laughed. "You could say that."

Could you get to the point in this century? She instantly chastised herself. The man sounded feeble.

"I don't mean to be rude, but how can I help you?"

"Your name's Tasha, right?" He didn't wait for her to answer. "Do you pronounce that with a hard 'a' like 'ate' or with a soft 'a' like 'ahhh'?"

The conversation was getting weirder by the minute. "Soft *a*," she replied.

"Tasha, I'm your father."

At that moment, in her mind, Tasha saw a runaway freight train suddenly hit a solid brick wall. The train cars bunched up, crumpled and twisted in odd angles. "Excuse me?"

"I'm your father," the man slowly repeated, as if she hadn't understood his words.

Her patience snapped. "I don't have a father."

"Darlin', I believe biology would disagree with you on that point." A wheezy, distinct cackle wafted through her phone. A cackle. He had a wild cackle. Like her.

The gravity of his words hit her full force. This man was claiming he was her father. A man her mother never spoke of, except to say their union had been a mistake. And that he wasn't worth wasting her breath on.

Tasha heard the microwave beep in the kitchen. Soon after, Zed reappeared. "Coffee's ready," he whispered.

Tasha nodded.

"I'm sorry—did you say your name was Van?" she asked the stranger.

"Vincent," he emphatically replied.

"Sorry. Vincent, can I get back with you?" She needed to process the bomb the man had just dropped in her lap.

"You promise to call me back?"

She paused. She didn't like to make empty promises. Giving her word was sacred. "Yes," she said finally. "I've got your number on my phone now."

"Okay. You have a good evening."

"You, too," she said. Even when she was irritated, her manners were always intact. She pressed the button to end the call.

"I'll be right there, Zed." She headed to the half bath, just under the stairwell. After closing the door, she leaned against it and tried to slow her erratic breathing. She felt like she'd been hit with a two-by-four.

She turned on the faucet and cupped her hands, gathering a pool of water. She splashed her face. Her earlier optimism and excitement at the possibilities of the New Year had taken a hit.

She'd always considered her father as good as dead. When she'd asked about him, wanting to know about the other half of herself, her mother had adamantly refused to speak much about him. Her mother could be stubborn. Tasha finally accepted he'd abandoned them and learned to live with his absence.

She tried to wrap her mind around the shocking call.

Could it have been a prank? Or a scammer?

She considered both ideas. But why would someone come from out of nowhere with such a claim? Especially after all these years.

Tasha patted her face dry with a towel. When she felt composed, she left the bathroom.

The aroma of the coffee filled the air. When she entered the living room, she saw Zed had lit candles. Soft R&B music poured from the house speakers.

While his thoughtful gesture touched her, it also had an odd effect. Tasha felt her composure seeping away. His kindness was like the last straw. It broke her.

"Tasha, what's wrong?"

She tried to speak, but only managed a croak. Fresh tears, like the gentle spray at the start of a storm, rolled down her cheeks.

Zed leaped toward her and wrapped her in his arms. His concern did her in. Sobs racked her body, and Zed held her until she was cried out.

"Wanna talk about it?" he gently asked.

"Can I reheat my coffee first?" She needed time to process the call.

He nodded. "Sure."

She warmed her coffee and joined him on the living room couch. After drawing in a steadying breath, she told Zed about the odd phone call.

"Oh, wow," he said.

"Tell me about it. I'm still in shock."

He studied her closely. "What are you going to do?"

"I promised to call him back."

His brow contorted. "You don't think it's some kind of scam, do you?"

"That did cross my mind. But what if it isn't? Don't I owe myself to at least check it out?"

"Tash, that's your choice to make."

"What would you do, if you were me?"

He stood and strolled to the crackling fireplace, then stretched his hands to warm them by the fire. "I'd contact him. I mean, it's possibly half of your DNA. That you know nothing about. You must have been curious all these years."

She nodded. "I was. But my mom always shut me down when I asked about him. After a while, I just gave up."

Zed's jaw tensed. "Do you think what your mom did was fair?"

Tasha instinctively knew he'd posed the inquiry as a question to be diplomatic. She guessed he already had an opinion on the matter.

"Probably not," she replied. "But when it comes to matters of the heart, things are rarely black-and-white."

Zed's head cocked back at her words. "True that." He rejoined her on the couch. "Can I ask one favor?"

"Sure," she said.

"If you decide to meet him, I want to go with you. And can you keep me on point about your conversations with him?"

"Zed, you don't have to do that." She was touched by his kindness, but hoped he didn't feel obligated to help her with her family mess.

"You're right. But I want to. You're my wife. I made a legal vow to look out for you. And I intend on keeping it. For as long as we're married."

Tasha started to argue. However, his stubborn expression stopped her. Was this what a true relationship was like—rock-solid commitment and caring? If so, she needed to steel her heart against being affected by his kindness and concern now, so it wouldn't hurt so bad when it abruptly ended.

Zed had stewed on the matter of the stranger's call until he finally convinced Tasha she should contact the man. She'd done so, and she'd had several conversations with Vincent. She discovered, to her surprise, that he resided in an assisted-living facility on the southeast side of Denver. Though he was in his fifties, fragile health and balance issues had necessitated he live somewhere he had access to 24-7 care. She had finally decided to go visit him.

She was unusually quiet on the drive there. Rather than fill the silence with conversation, he was glad to leave her to her thoughts. Having lost of both his parents, he felt it was important for her to learn more about the man who claimed to be her father, as well as process all the emotions related to the news.

The first thing that hit his nostrils when they walked into Whispering Pines assisted-living facility was the strong smell of bleach. Tasha gazed at him, her expression asking for reassurance.

"I got you," he whispered.

She finally nodded, and they went to the information desk and asked for directions to Vincent's room. The receptionist seemed surprised when they mentioned his name. But she quickly hid her reaction and pasted on an obligatory smile.

Zed had the feeling Vincent didn't get many, if any, visitors.

As they walked down the winding white brick corridor that was bathed in fluorescent light, Tasha repeatedly flexed her hands, a sign, he guessed, that her anxiety was mounting. He understood. This man could be her father and could be a missing piece, the other half of who she was as a person.

He prayed the whole thing wasn't a scam. But if Vincent was truly her father, it wasn't going to be an easy road when deep-rooted hurt and myriad other feelings arose, like sediment from an ocean bottom.

They finally arrived at Vincent's room. Tasha took a deep breath.

He went into the room ahead of her, like a protective shield. "Vincent Taliferro?" he tentatively asked.

"Yes, sirree, that would be me," a craggy voice answered. A medium-size man sat hunched over in a wheelchair.

Zed shot out a hand. "I'm Zed Evans. And this is my wife, Tasha."

Zed moved out of the way, unblocking Tasha's view. When the man saw Tasha, upturned eyes that mirrored her own soaked her in like a sponge.

The sudden violent sobs from the huddled-up man shocked Zed, and he guessed Tasha, too. Vincent's thin arms, cloaked in a pea green sweater and orange T-shirt, opened wide.

Tasha looked Zed's way, as if she wasn't sure what to do. He subtly nodded, directing her toward Vincent.

She headed across the room and gave the gentleman an awkward embrace.

Vincent trembled as Tasha held him. After she released him, Vincent motioned for Zed to approach.

Zed obeyed, giving Vincent a light hug and fist pound, noting the gentleman smelled like a combination of soap, cheap cologne and mint mouthwash.

Upon releasing the man, he joined Tasha, who sat in one of the two dull brown tweed chairs across from Vincent's bed.

Tears baptized the gentleman's face.

Zed retrieved a handkerchief from his pocket and handed it to the man.

"Thank you," Vincent said. "I'm out of tissues." He wiped his wet cheeks. When he was composed again, he observed Tasha quietly. "I see so much of your mother in you. Not just the physical things, but the sweet spirit that always shined from her eyes."

A rogue protective thought assaulted Zed at the comment. *If her mother was so sweet, why did you abandon them?*

"Thank you," Tasha replied.

"Mr. Taliferro, you can imagine what a shock this has been for my wife to hear from you," he said.

Vincent nodded. "I can understand that."

"How did you know my mother?" Tasha asked.

Vincent's eyes narrowed in apparent curiosity. "She never mentioned me?"

"No," Tasha replied.

Hurt rolled across the man's face, as if he'd been punched.

"Although that's hard to hear, I guess it makes sense," he finally said. "Violet-Sage's heart was never really mine."

Tasha waited for Vincent to explain the curious remark.

"Your mom and I met in grade school. We lived in the same neighborhood. In high school we had algebra class together. I was never good at math and she tutored me. I was good in English lit, which she was not, so I helped her with her writing. We often did our homework at your grandparents' house. She and my sister, Karen, were friends." He halted. "I'm guessing you knew her home life wasn't the best."

Hearing Vincent's words, Zed's heart ached for Tasha and the dysfunction and pain that ran through her family like an errant thread.

Tasha nodded. "Mama talked about her dad being an alcoholic. He was both verbally and physically abusive. But my grandmother, fearful she couldn't financially make it on her own, stayed with him. Just when she finally could no longer endure his treatment and made plans to leave him, he died of cirrhosis of the liver."

A woeful look crossed Vincent's face. "Yes, your mother and grandmother went through a lot. Such a shame. They deserved so much better." He sighed. "Violet-Sage was my first love," Vincent continued. "Unfortunately for me, her heart belonged to somebody else. I waited patiently. When her boyfriend broke up with her before going into the military, I made my move. She was vulnerable, and I knew she cared for me. Your mama was so hungry for love. Starving for it, really. And I just happened to be there. I wanted to comfort her and show her how much I loved her."

Zed contrasted his mother's starvation for attention from his dad against Vincent's desire to fill the hole in Tasha's mother's heart. If only his father had been like Vincent.

Vincent continued. "We were together one night. I was a senior in high school, about to be a first-generation college student with a basketball scholarship, when she told me she was pregnant. I'm not proud of the fact that I acted immaturely. I could barely take care of myself and I saw my future going down the drain. I was just a kid myself. Although I loved her, I loved myself more and I selfishly chose my future."

Zed sighed, sorry to learn that Tasha's dad had been more like his own father than he wished. It was amazing to him the domino effect their decisions had on their children.

"Violet-Sage had every right to cut me off and want to have nothing to do with me. A few years later, through my sister, Karen, I learned that she had the chance to get back with her boyfriend. She wanted to be honest about what happened with me, but when she told him, it ended their relationship. I felt awful.

"After college I found her and offered to marry her. She refused to have anything to do with me. I now realize why she had to cut me off. I think, in addition to my selfish actions, she refused me partly because of what happened with her parents. She told me once that your grandmother married your grandfather not out of love, but out of desperation and fear of being alone. Though she cared for me, she didn't love me. And because of how her parents' relationship turned out, I believe she didn't want to take any chances of repeating history."

"Did you ever have a family?" Tasha asked.

"I was married. For twenty-nine years. My wife, Miriam, died of cancer six years ago. She wasn't able to have children."

"I'm sorry," Tasha said.

"Me, too, sir," Zed added.

Vincent dipped his head in apparent acknowledgment of their words. "Thank you both. Miriam was a good woman. We didn't have the fireworks kind of love that lights up the sky. But we had a solid relationship."

Zed marveled at Vincent's almost poetic way of putting things.

Watching Tasha as Vincent began telling some childhood stories, Zed could sense she was overwhelmed. She was probably on system overload and needed to retreat, to process and absorb everything.

He turned to her father.

"Mr. Taliferro, it has been a pleasure to meet you. As you might imagine, this has been a lot for my wife to take in. Can we arrange to meet another time?"

Vincent gave them a sheepish look. "I'm sorry. I've had a little more time to absorb this news. Just after my sister told me about your mother's death a year ago, she mentioned that she'd spoken with Violet before her death and that your mother had made her peace over the past and she'd forgiven me. I struggled with whether I should find you. I knew there was a chance if you knew about me from your mother that you might hate me, and I'd risk rejection. I finally decided it was worth the risk to know you." He paused. She saw fear flicker in his eyes. "Promise me you will come back, and we won't lose touch?"

"I promise," Tasha said.

He thinks she'll be like her mother and cut him off, too, Zed thought. *If only he knew the Tasha that I've come to know, the woman who has a heart as huge as Texas.* Would it be easy? Probably not. But he guessed Tasha would ultimately come around.

Zed reached in his wallet, took out money and gave it to Vincent. "Stash this for your needs." He added a friendly wink.

Vincent eagerly took the money. "Much obliged. It will go to good use. Some of my socks have got so many holes in them, somebody said they could pass for sandals." Vincent chuckled at his own joke. Until his laughter escalated into a coughing frenzy. Zed got him a glass of water before they left.

On the ride home, he decided not to pressure

Tasha to talk, in case she didn't want to. She finally looked his way.

"I always took pride in how tight me and my mother were. I'm sad she kept what happened with my father from me. My feelings are all over the map right now. I grieve for my mother's lost love, and I'm both sad and angry at Vincent. I'm sorry for his unreciprocated love and the lost time he never got with me. But I know he's partially to blame for everything, because of his irresponsibility." She paused and looked out the window at the moving landscape. This time she didn't turn back to him when she spoke. "What I don't get is why he didn't fight to get to know me."

Zed had a feeling her statement had subtext that went beyond what her father had done, but since he had no answers, he reached out to take her hand and held it to let her know she was not alone.

Chapter Eleven

For the next several days Tasha had a few phone conversations with Vincent, before deciding to visit him again. This time she went alone to have a more intimate conversation with him. Beyond the shock of meeting her father, several new realizations hit her. For one, a whole new world had opened for her. She would be able to put some of the puzzle pieces of her life together.

She was grateful Zed had come with her to meet Vincent. His strength and steady presence had helped her get through the difficult meeting.

What am I going to do when he's no longer around? Something in her heart pinged. *Danger, girl. You're getting too used to his presence in your life.* Anger erupted in her. *Lord, what's wrong with me? Why was I never worthy to have someone like Zed permanently in my life? Why am I always the one standing outside the candy shop pressing my nose against the window, while everybody else gets to go inside?*

Vincent—she still felt shy about calling him her father—was alone in the world, as she was. His tiny room in the dingy facility appeared to be sparse and lonely. She had so many questions. How was he able to afford the place? What had his occupation been? She also wanted to know more about his childhood.

She needed to have a long talk with God. In the Bible, He encouraged his children to pour their hearts out to Him. To cast their cares on Him. In the meantime, she needed to sort her feelings about her visit with Vincent. And consider the questions his stories raised about her mother's life.

As she drove to meet Vincent, Tasha looked up at the sky and imagined beyond the stars and planets, to heaven. "Lord, thank You for bringing Vincent—my father—into my life. Although this is a shock, I know You've got me. Let me be a blessing to him." Maybe God wanted Vincent to be a blessing to her, as well.

Grateful for thin traffic, she enjoyed the peaceful ride to her father's facility. She made good time, which was great because her curiosity about her mother's love life was now practically eating her up. Tasha whipped her Mini Cooper into the assisted-living facility parking lot. She hopped out of the car and was halfway to the front door when she realized she'd forgotten the things she'd brought for him.

Returning to the vehicle, she got her shopping bag filled with puzzle books, Mallomars cookies, peanut butter and Ritz crackers, and strawberry Twizzlers. Her father had mentioned these were some of his favorite things in their recent phone conversation.

Although she knew she should have strongly cautioned him against the junk food, these small things brought him happiness. She decided to give the candy to the nurses to parse out to her father, so he didn't go overboard on the sweets.

She found him sitting watching old *I Love Lucy* reruns. Like father, like daughter, she realized with a small amount of pleasure. When she entered the room, his saddle-brown face, with deep-grooved wrinkles, lit up.

"Hi," she said shyly. She still hadn't been able to call him Father yet.

"Love Nugget," he cried affectionately. She'd learned, from hearing him speak about the nurses and techs, that he liked giving acquaintances nicknames.

"I brought you some things." She handed him the bag she'd brought.

He surveyed his loot, a grin curving his full lips. "Thank you, darlin'."

She sat across from him and his attention momentarily returned to the TV show. They both laughed at Lucy's wild antics.

Tasha considered how to bring up the subject of her mother's love life. She cleared her throat several times. "Vincent, may I ask you a question about my mother?"

He looked her way and paused. Tasha wondered if it bothered him that she still called him by his name.

"Sure. Ask away."

"You said my mother had one great love. Did you know him?"

Instead of answering right away, her father ripped open a package of beef jerky he'd retrieved from a side drawer. He took a bite and slowly chewed, closing his eyes in apparent pleasure.

Was he purposely taking his time answering?

"I didn't know him," he finally announced.

She tried to curb her disappointment. Maybe it was better that she didn't know this information.

"I didn't know him, personally, that is. Your mom knew how I felt about her. I believe she didn't discuss her relationship with me because of that."

Tasha held her breath and waited for more information from Vincent.

"Most of what I know is secondhand. Through my sister, Karen. Like I mentioned, she and your mother were friends. I know he was a veteran. And that your mother had wanted him to marry her. But he refused." Vincent shook his head. "Broke your mama's heart."

His dark eyes studied her, as if he was trying to decide something. "To be honest, I think him not wanting to marry her was a cop-out. If he really loved her, he should have moved heaven and earth to be with her."

Tasha's heart pinged at his words. What did it say about her that no man had ever wanted to move heaven and earth to be with her?

"Sometimes I hear these young nurses 'round here talking about wondering if a guy cares for them." He shook his head woefully. "I say, ninety-nine percent of the time, if you got to ask that question, you got your answer."

A bird flitting in the bushes outside the window temporarily caught his attention. "You know, that's why I'm so proud of you, Tasha. You waited for love. And like the young people say, you made sure he put a ring on it. I see too many of these young gals settling for so much less than they're worth. I'm gonna use you as an example when I talk to the nurses. You waited and were blessed with true love."

An ache started at the pit of her stomach. She needed to change the subject fast, before both sorrow and guilt over her fake situation overtook her. "What kind of man was my mother's love?"

"My sister said he was the life of the party. He was smart, funny and charming."

On the television, the music for *I Dream of Jeannie* started. Vincent turned up the volume. "I love old television shows. Cheesy as they are."

Tasha wondered if his abrupt change of the subject might mean that all her questions were hurting him. She decided to go along with the subject change. "I love old shows, too."

"How would you know about these shows, young lady?"

"Reruns."

They both hummed the theme song along with the television. At the end of the melody, they chuckled.

Conflicting emotions swirled within her. There was the sorrow at the loss of years she and her father could never get back. There was anger at him for not fighting to find her. And finally, there was anger at her mother for being too proud to take help from the man.

"Is something wrong?" Vincent asked.

Tasha shook free of her reverie. "I'm sorry. I need to get going."

"But you just got here." His eyes held a silent plea for her to stay.

Her emotions were raw and eggshell thin. "I'll

stay longer next time. Promise." Still shy about affection toward him, she approached and gently squeezed his leathery brown hand. "Take care of yourself. Call me if you need anything."

Vincent nodded in silent agreement."

"Oh—there is one other thing I remember my sister telling me about your mother's beau," Vincent said.

She tried not to laugh at her father's outdated term for her mother's first love. "What's that?" she asked.

"Karen said he lived in a house in that swanky Avenue Parkway neighborhood, in a purple Victorian."

Tasha suppressed a gasp. Zed's Victorian was purple and in Avenue Parkway. And Aunt Zora's letter had mentioned rumors of Zed's dad being involved with a childhood sweetheart. A further shocking thought came to her—had her and her mother's visits to the Victorian been more than coincidental? Had the place they'd assumed belonged to a family who led idyllic lives been more of an illusion than she thought? And would the knowledge she possibly had further shatter that illusion—and possibly Zed's heart?

Zed sat in the dark. Through the window he could see the navy blue sky, illuminated by a fingernail moon. Outside, crickets put on a free orchestra.

Tasha had retired to bed early. He could understand why. He knew the past week must have been overwhelming for her after meeting her father.

He wrung his hands several times. It was a nervous gesture from his childhood. He sympathized with Tasha and had been glad to be with her for the first meeting with the man who claimed to be her father.

He thought of the man that had rocked Tasha's world. Something about the situation troubled Zed. Was Vincent really her father? Did he have ulterior motives? He wouldn't tell Tasha, but he might just do a little bit of investigating. Because there was one thing he did know—Tasha was one of the sweetest women he'd ever met. And he'd do whatever it took within his power to protect her. It was critical that he talk to Vincent as soon as possible. If Tasha was in danger of being taken advantage of, he wanted to nip it in the bud. He'd give the guy a chance before he took more drastic measures, such as possibly hiring a private investigator.

Zed grabbed his phone and digitally penciled a time on his calendar the next day to drop by the assisted-living facility.

The next morning, after consuming a quick

drive-through breakfast, he headed into the office early to get some tasks done and knock out a few committee meeting agendas in preparation for the new semester. Doing so would help make up for the time he'd planned to leave the office to meet Tasha's dad. He was amazed at how fast the morning sped by.

When he finally maneuvered his truck into a parking space at Vincent's facility, he cut the engine, took a deep breath and sat quietly for a moment.

His heart would break for Tasha if his suspicions were true that the man who claimed to be her father, which was still questionable, had ulterior motives for contacting her. He didn't know how he would tell her about Vincent, if his inkling was correct. He knew she was fragile.

First, he was bound and determined to find out if Vincent was truly her father. He planned to suggest a blood test. Vincent's reaction would be telling.

Zed finally exited his vehicle and strolled to the facility's entrance. He dipped his head in polite greeting to the front desk receptionist. She returned a kind smile that lit up her brown eyes as she offered him the sign-in book.

Zed scribbled his name and headed for Vincent's room. He knocked to be polite.

Vincent was sitting at a small table by the only

window in the room. A plant with both robust green leaves and a few curling brown ones sat next to a checkerboard. The man was evidently playing checkers with himself.

Surprise lit Vincent's features when he spotted Zed in the doorway, and Zed guessed he wasn't used to guests. "Well, hello, young man."

"Hey, sir." Regardless of his suspicions, his mother had taught him to always be a gentleman. He crossed the room and gave Vincent a fist pound.

Vincent shoved the game board aside and looked past Zed. "Is my daughter with you?"

Zed shook his head. "I thought you and I might talk."

He mustered his most serious, normally intimidating expression. He didn't want the man to think he was a pushover.

"You can probably imagine what a bombshell your news was to Tasha. She is a very trusting, kindhearted soul. I, however, am a little more wary. Is there something you want to tell me?"

Vincent's watery dark eyes looked past him out the window.

"I should have known you'd play hardball. It's obvious you care for my daughter very much."

Wow. My acting skills must be better than I thought. He squelched any consideration that Vincent could have seen anything more.

"I admit that finding Tasha was a bit selfish of me," Vincent announced. "I need her emotional support, and to be honest, I thought a little financial help would be nice." He ran his thick, withered fingers over his gray, buzz-cut hair.

To Zed's surprise, Vincent's eyes filled with tears. "I can honestly say I've enjoyed getting to know her," Vincent continued. "Like seeing a mirror of myself, in some ways. Something about her kinda takes you by surprise, you know? She's a sweet little thing. So kind."

Zed sat in one of the chairs across from Vincent's bed. The man's words about Tasha struck a chord in him. But this wasn't the confession he was expecting. He bolstered himself up and cut to the chase. "How do you feel about taking a blood test?"

Vincent's expression remained confident. "I'm ready and willing. Anytime. I have nothing to hide. Private investigator, background check, you name it, I'll do it."

The air seeped out of Zed's lungs, like water through a sieve. While he should have been glad his suspicions that the man was a scammer were wrong, he realized he'd been terrified he was right.

"You must love her very much," Vincent said. "You're very protective of her."

Zed rocked back on his heels. The unexpected

statement took him off guard. He struggled to get his game face on. "She is my wife," he managed to eke out.

His words sounded weak even to his own ears as soon as they spilled out of his mouth. He abruptly rose. The conversation was getting a little too hot for him to handle. "Nice to see you again, sir."

He shook Vincent's hand and headed for the door. But before exiting, he halted and turned back toward the man. Vincent had been wrong for having any ulterior motive besides wanting to get to know his daughter. Period. She'd been hurt and used enough. But Zed still felt sorry for him and committed to pray for the man. "If it helps, Mr. Taliferro, I can assure you that getting to know your daughter is worth far more than any monetary gain. She's priceless."

Vincent's eyes widened in surprise.

"Take care of yourself, sir," Zed said.

In the truck on the way home, when he recalled his final words to Vincent about Tasha, his heart raced. He reminded himself that their relationship had an end date. Period.

Chapter Twelve

It's Valentine's Day. My last holiday as a married woman. Tasha tried to push aside her mixed feelings about what had once been her favorite holiday—until she'd been dumped on Valentine's, by text, at a five-star restaurant. And, to add insult to injury, she'd been left to pay the hefty bill, when her boyfriend Reggie had dismissed himself before dessert to head to the restroom and never returned. After unanswered calls and texts, later that night she'd received his breakup text. *Boy, could she pick 'em.*

After the incident she'd finally concluded that she wasn't going to let some deadbeat boyfriend ruin the beauty of the holiday. She decided to fight to reignite her joy for the day by celebrating love in all its forms.

She hoped Zed had planned something for the day, since they'd celebrated the other two holidays of their faux marriage in a special way.

But he'd said nothing about Valentine's Day, even though he'd promised her, as a Christmas gift, three wonderful holidays.

Tasha guessed Valentine's Day might be a hot-button item for Zed. Maybe he knew how much it meant to most women, and avoiding it was his way of keeping distance between them—a silent method of letting her know his resolve was airtight to not get romantically involved. For all she knew, he might just buy her a greeting card and chocolates. Not exactly original, but enough to meet the bare minimum requirement for the day for most ladies.

Tasha climbed out of bed and tiptoed to the window, enjoying the way the old floors creaked against her weight. She pushed back the white lace curtains and let daylight pour in.

A whishing sound caught her attention, and she turned just in time to see an envelope slide under the door.

"What in the world?"

She retrieved the pristine white envelope. The front had a picture of a heart with a crisscross line through it. She opened it and found a note in Zed's squiggly handwriting, which read, "Happy Un-Valentine's Day."

Tasha crinkled her nose at the odd card. She didn't know whether to be happy or offended.

She washed up and went downstairs, looking

around to see what Zed might have planned, considering his odd note. Would there be crushed candy hearts and signs that read "down with love"?

She found him at the entrance to the kitchen. He blocked her way. "Hey, Tash."

She tried to read his mysterious expression. "Thanks, I think, for the note."

"You're un-welcome," Zed said.

Tasha laughed. "Okay, enough already. What's going on?"

Zed's eyebrows wiggled. "In time, my sweet."

"Nice pun. You're certainly on point today. Or not," she joked.

He took a towel and put it on his crooked arm, like a high-class maître d'. "Your table is ready, mademoiselle." He led her to the kitchen table and pulled out a chair for her.

On the table was a plate with heart-shaped pancakes covered with strawberries and a dollop of whipped cream.

"Oh, wow." Tasha sat and noticed he didn't have a plate. "Aren't you joining me?"

"This is your day. It's all about you. I've got an unforgettable day planned for you."

Zed, in his old-man pajamas that she'd only seen men wear in old movies, with those mesmerizing eyes and smile that shamed the sun, made her heart miss a step in its regular dance in her chest.

"Okay, if this is my day and I can have anything I want, I'd like you to join me for breakfast."

Something flickered in Zed's eyes, but it quickly dissipated. "Your wish is my command." He bowed grandly. "So *boom*. Keepin' it real, here's the plan for the day. I know Valentine's Day is a messed-up holiday for you. Because of the dude who shall remain nameless, who broke up with you on one of your most favorite holidays, we're going to undo your bad memories of the day from your past."

Tasha's insides felt like melted chocolate. However, she put on a steely front. "Nice," she replied.

"And because I'm a master list maker and planner, here's our itinerary for the day." He removed a folded piece of paper from his robe pocket and handed it to her.

Tasha unfolded the paper and read the activities. They seemed random and unrelated. "How should I dress for the day?"

Zed headed to the stove to apparently make his pancakes. "As you wish, my chocolate drop."

She chuckled. "What color should I wear?"

"Purple. Your favorite color," he replied.

She hid her shock and surprise that he'd remembered the small detail about her.

Zed added small iron templates of hearts to the skillet and poured in batter. Once they were flipped and done, he prepared his plate similarly to hers, then poured a glass of milk before joining her with his meal. He immediately took a hefty swig of the beverage.

Tasha stifled a giggle.

"What?" Zed asked.

"You've got a milk mustache." Without thinking, she reached over and ran her forefinger over his upper lip to remove the temporary mustache. She was so close, she felt the feathery waves of his warm, mouthwash-scented breath. The air in her lungs hitched. She sat back so fast, she almost lost her balance. Thankfully, she was able to grab the edge of the table to settle herself. Embarrassed, she felt her face flush.

She hoped Zed would laugh it off. But his expression was serious. Unsolved mysteries swirled in his light eyes.

Tasha quickly finished her meal. "I'd better get ready, if we're going to stay on schedule," she said.

He nodded but said nothing.

Tasha rummaged through her closet, trying to decide what to wear. She usually wore red to celebrate the day for lovers. But she liked Zed's suggestion of her favorite color, so she chose her favorite full-length purple velour dress. Its simple lines complemented her figure, and the color flattered her warm chocolate skin tone.

When she went downstairs to meet Zed, he whistled through his teeth. "Very nice," he said.

"Thanks." Tasha got her coat, gloves and winter scarf from the hall closet.

As they walked to the garage, she quizzed Zed. "So your first appointment says 'therapy.' Does this involve me pouring my heart out on a couch, and do I need tissues?"

"You'll see," he said. Zed opened the passenger side of the truck for her.

"Well, alrighty, then. Can you at least tell me where we're going?"

"Littleton."

Tasha's heart warmed with pleasure. She loved quaint, small Colorado towns. Littleton, Colorado, was one of her favorites. The place retained its historic look with old vintage buildings, mixed with midcentury modern structures. She'd read that the town had really boomed just after World War II when the aerospace/aviation industry had picked the small town as a major hub.

As Zed maneuvered on the highway, Tasha observed him. He seemed oblivious to her as he belted out some song on the radio. To his credit, the man had many good qualities, but singing was not one of them. He was so bad, in a way he was good. You couldn't say he didn't pour his heart into it.

What surprised her most about him was his listening skills. She was sure she hadn't mentioned her love for Littleton more than once in passing conversation. However, he seemed to remember even the little things that she loved.

She was so used to guys who made themselves the center of the world. They talked about themselves incessantly. They may or may not have asked her about herself. If they did, generally it was an afterthought. Like throwing a dog a bone.

When they arrived in Littleton, Zed parked on one of the side streets and they exited his truck. As Tasha walked alongside him, she peered west, enjoying the amazing view of the mountains. Glorious, voluminous white clouds dotted the sky over the mountain peaks. The contrast of the dark, navy blue, craggy range made for a beautiful sight.

"I'd say they're Winsome today," Zed declared.

"Huh?"

"I give the mountains names, depending on how they look. Today they're lovely, engaging—Winsome."

Tasha smiled. "I like that. I may steal your idea."

He produced a deep-throated chuckle. "No need to steal. I'll gladly lend it to you."

Tasha walked in silence, curious where Zed

was leading her. Although she was familiar with Littleton, she'd yet to explore all the downtown's quaint shops and businesses.

When Zed finally stopped in front of a storefront, she nearly bumped into him.

"Here we are," he announced.

Tasha looked at the sign above the business. It read Chocolate Therapy.

She giggled with delight. "Seriously!"

Zed grinned. "Yes, ma'am. It's just what the doctor ordered."

She wanted to dance on the sidewalk with glee, but she reined herself in. As they entered the shop, the varying smells of chocolate nearly took her breath away.

"Pick whatever you'd like," he said.

"There's so much! This will be hard!"

"I believe in you."

"Ha!" Tasha's eyes roamed the place. She considered her strategy and decided to start in one corner of the wall of candy and circle the place.

She finally settled on a yummy dark chocolate bar with marshmallows. They sat at one of the circular high tables. "You have to try some, too," she told Zed.

"Sure," he said. "But first—" He searched his pocket and pulled out what looked like another greeting card. He handed it to her.

The envelope was purple. "What's this?"

"Look and see."

She opened the card. Admiring the ornate art-work, she ran her hands over the calligraphy. Her heart trilled at his small gesture of picking such a beautiful card for her. Nobody had ever considered her so thoroughly. And it was possible nobody ever would again.

Zed held his breath as Tasha reviewed his greeting card.

"May I read it aloud?" she asked.

"Sure."

Tasha cleared her throat and started to read. "'Tasha, I hope this "therapy" helps replace the bitter taste left in your mouth from your past dark Valentine's Day, where you once were led to feel unwanted and unloved. I hope you know the sweet things that make you not only unique, but also special, such as your weird-cute laugh that gives a hyena a run for its money, your large heart that blesses others and deserves to be blessed, too, your love of history, all things chocolate, onesies and retro TV shows, and your beauty, both inside and out. The guy that let you go on this day made a huge, ginormous mistake. I hope my therapy prescription helps heal your ailing heart. Or at least brings a little sunshine to replace that dark day. Happy Un-Valentine's Day —Zed.'" She locked eyes with him.

"Oh, Zed, it's one of the most beautiful cards I've ever received!"

He was surprised to feel both touched and shy. His father had disdained overly emotional displays, which made it hard, since his mother had always been a firecracker of emotion. His natural inclination was to play down the moment with Tasha. The best way he knew how was to deflect things. He started to hurriedly pack her stash of chocolate. "I hate to rush you, but we'll be late for our next task for the day if you don't hurry."

Tasha seemed surprised at the sudden change of mood, but she complied. She took the itinerary he'd made for her from her purse. "Next up, let's see—'Cupcake Brigade,'" she read. She wrinkled her cute little nose. "More sugar?" she asked as they exited the restaurant.

"Not exactly. You'll see," he replied.

Once they were seated in his truck, he whipped the vehicle onto Santa Fe, one of the main streets in Littleton. Shortly thereafter, they stopped at Aspen Grove, a huge strip mall of stores.

"I'll be right back," he said. He leaped from the vehicle and disappeared into a cupcake shop. Ten minutes later he exited with three large pink boxes.

Zed sat the boxes in the truck bed before re-entering the vehicle.

"Three huge boxes of cupcakes. Dare I ask?" she said.

"You'll see."

Forty minutes later they were in north Denver. He pulled up to a women's shelter called Ruth's Promise. When he cut the engine, he turned to Tasha.

"I know you have a heart for the less fortunate, from the vision you shared when we first met of wanting to use part of the proceeds from your business to help others. Since Valentine's Day celebrates love in all its forms, I thought you might like blessing some women and their families with gourmet cupcakes to let them know they matter and are special to God, too.

"Plus, by giving instead of just receiving on this day, I hope the joy will replace the sorrow you felt at giving your heart, but never receiving back. I know it sounds like a paradox, but sometimes giving can make us happier and more fulfilled."

He gazed at her, hoping that he'd guessed right and that this would be an idea she would like. Had he read her right? If he was wrong, the day could quickly tank, which was the last thing he wanted.

Tasha looked stunned. "Thank you," she said softly. "I love your idea."

He sighed with relief. "You're very welcome.

Now, c'mon, Tash. I've arranged with the director to distribute the cupcakes to the ladies and their kids, too." As he started to exit the truck, he stopped. "Oh, and I've also got some Valentine's Day cards in the glove compartment. Could you grab those?"

Over the next twenty minutes Zed was happy to witness how grateful the women in the shelter were at his and Tasha's small gesture. It brought many of them to tears, including Tasha.

"That was so precious," Tasha said when they returned to the vehicle after distributing the treats. "I think you made those ladies' day, week, maybe even year."

"They deserved to know they are seen and valued," Zed said.

She observed him for a long moment, seeming touched by his words, but then she returned her attention to the itinerary. "So next is a break for the afternoon, then dinner plans, but you don't say where we're going for dinner." She cocked her head to one side and wrinkled her nose in apparent curiosity. "Are you taking me to Shanahan's, where I was stood up on Valentine's Day, to make up for it?"

"Time will tell," he said.

"What should I wear?"

"Clothes would be good," Zed quipped.

"Zed, be serious."

"Dress attire," he replied.

"Okay." She watched the passing landscape before turning back to him. "You realize it's our last holiday as a married couple."

Did he hear wistfulness and melancholy in her voice? Had he gone a little too overboard? He still needed to keep his distance so that they could make a clean and easy break when their arrangement ended.

Later, when Tasha appeared at the top of the steps for their dinner date, she wore an emerald green full-length dress, with glittery dewdrop diamond earrings and shoes that matched the dress.

"Wow," he said.

"Right back at you," she said. "You spit-shine pretty good in that tux there, mister."

He chuckled, offered his arm and escorted her to the truck.

Mrs. Talmadge, their elderly next-door neighbor, was on her porch as they walked toward the car. She gave a hardy whistle.

He smiled and graciously dipped his head in response.

When they finally were in the truck and on the way to their destination, Tasha tried to get out of him where they were going. It didn't work.

As he drove, he snuck quick peeks at her when he thought she wasn't aware of his scrutiny. He tried to keep his cool. He wanted to drink in her loveliness slowly, like a sumptuous meal. Although she wasn't a traditional beauty, she had a unique, quirky loveliness that took his breath away. The kindness, compassion and humor that gleamed from her dark eyes, the sweet smile that reflected her generosity and kindness, all added up to something amazing. The green dress she wore complemented her warm brown skin and dark brown hair with sandy highlights, which she'd piled on top of her head so that it fell in a cascade of curls. He liked how she'd added wispy tendrils around the nape of her neck and ears.

I'll miss her. The rebel thought caught him off guard. Where had it come from? He grit his jaw in stubborn determination against the idea. He hadn't needed anyone since his mother died. And he didn't now.

"Is something wrong?" Tasha asked.

Man. She can read me like nobody else.

"No. I'm fine," he said. He turned on the radio, hoping the music would distract him, and concentrated on how Tasha would react at their dinner date location. It would certainly be interesting. It would either be great or a total bust.

Just after a traffic light, Zed put on his right turn signal and entered the parking lot of the restaurant.

Tasha's dark eyes turned into wide orbs of

amazement. "Zed. Seriously? What's going on? A fast-food restaurant?" Tasha cried.

Zed grinned. He parked, exited and opened her door for her, then offered his arm to escort her again.

Tasha's straight-ahead stare told him she was purposely attempting to ignore some snickers as they walked into the restaurant looking like Ken and Barbie headed to the Oscars.

"The sky's the limit. Order whatever you'd like."

"Big spender," she replied.

To his amazement, although she was surprised, she didn't seem offended or upset. That told him a lot about her. He'd dated women that would have been furious at his move. But Tasha was being a good sport.

She's one in a million.

Tasha ordered a Happy Meal. She patted the little box when she got it. "This way I'll have a memento of this day," she joked.

He ordered a quarter pounder with cheese meal, with a strawberry shake.

They found seats. A few toddlers, supervised by their parents, ran with abandon down the restaurant aisles. One kid saw them, stopped with his mouth agape and pointed them out to his parents.

A wistful expression rolled across Tasha's face. "When I was a kid, our big treat was to eat out once a month. My mother would always ask where I wanted to go. Why she did so, I'll never know, because I always said the same thing," she said.

"A fast-food place?" Zed asked.

"How'd you know?"

"I have my ways," he said. "Secret intel."

"I'm thinking more an educated guess."

Zed chuckled. "Busted."

They laughed and joked through the meal. When they were done, he produced her final Un-Valentine's card.

"Why, thank you," she said. She opened the card. "Should I read it aloud?"

"Your choice," he said.

She cleared her throat and started. "'Tasha, I'm guessing this wasn't the gourmet meal you were expecting. But since this is Un-Valentine's Day, and we're undoing your past Valentine's Day disaster, I wanted to take you somewhere normal. Because it's not just about celebrating someone on a certain day. You deserve to be celebrated every day, not only with fireworks and expensive meals, but in the simple, plain times and moments. Times that are real and true. You were stood up at a fancy restaurant and made to feel less than nothing. I wanted to dress up and take you somewhere simple and make you feel like the queen you are. You are worthy of knowing you're special all the time—'"

Crystal tears spilled down her cheeks. "I'm sorry," she cried.

"No apologies needed."

She swiped her eyes with her hands. "This is the best Un-Valentine's Day I've ever had. And this meal is more special to me than dining at a five-star restaurant. Because of you." Tasha's sable eyes bore into him. Her lips parted as if she wanted to say more. She paused, as if trying to decide something. "I see what your mom and aunt meant about you."

He broke eye contact with her and dramatically sucked the last of his shake, like an overeager child. Had he made a mistake? Was she getting too close to him? He'd wanted to make her day special. Had he gone too far?

They finished up and headed out to the truck. On the way home, Tasha was lit up like a Christmas tree. He tried to keep his eyes on the road, but when he took quick glances her way, her beauty and effervescence gleamed like a diamond. She chattered like a magpie. He was glad for that. It gave him time to think. He'd wanted to bless her, but Zed worried she might have misinterpreted his actions to mean more than they did.

When they got home, Tasha suggested they change into their pajamas and make popcorn balls. She said it was a quirky fun thing her mother did for Valentine's Day when Tasha was a kid. Tasha shared the recipe with him of mixing corn syrup, popcorn and M&M's to form balls.

After they were done eating the sweet treat, Tasha stopped him as they headed up the stairs. The moonlight, shining through the stained-glass window, caressed her face. "Thank you," she said, clutching her chest over her heart, "for one of the most amazing days of my life." Her lips quivered.

Zed's heart pounded in his chest. All this time, while he'd wondered whether she'd fall for him, she wasn't the one he should have been worried about. He felt as old as Moses and at the same time like a young, scared boy. "It's not fair, you know," he whispered.

Tasha gave him a curious look. "What?"

"That the moon's even trying to compete with you. 'Cause it's a lost cause. No contest."

He gently cupped her face in his hands. Her skin felt like satin under his fingers. Alarm bells went off in his head. He shouldn't have touched her. He attempted to back off, but some invisible force, like a magnet, drew him closer. Her full lips called to him. He bit his lip against the invitation. However, with dismay, he realized the moon wasn't the only one possibly fighting a lost cause. His mouth covered hers.

* * *

Tasha awakened to the sweet, salty taste of the popcorn and the memory of Zed's kiss from the night before still on her lips.

For a moment she wondered if she'd dreamed the wonderful day before, as well as Zed's kiss. Upon realizing it was real, she marveled. Had last night's events been a game changer for her and Zed? The way he'd kissed her, with utter tenderness, yet determination, as well, spoke volumes. She watched birds sing, flutter and dance outside her window, feeling as if she had wings, too.

She wanted to open up to Zed, to show him every part of her heart and who she was. A sharp pain pinged in her chest. Memories of when she'd done so before and ended up with a broken heart invaded her thoughts.

Zed might not have confessed his feelings aloud, but could his kiss have communicated that he felt something for her? If she was vulnerable and confessed how she was feeling, would she be putting their new connection in jeopardy forever? Was Zed different or was he just like all the other men that ultimately didn't feel as she did and abandoned her?

She wrestled with her thoughts during breakfast. When Zed joined her for cereal, he informed her he'd be holed up in his makeshift office most of the day. He told her about the challenge of dealing with students and community protests over the university's consideration of tearing down a beloved historic building, Lincoln Hall. He'd been charged with coming up with a proposal to address the issue to present to the chancellor.

"The thing of it is, I get the students' perspective. I'm a big historic architecture buff. It's part of the reason I became an architecture professor. Lincoln Hall certainly is beautiful and has a wonderful legacy at the school. But it's old and the continual repairs are costly. I understand the community and students. Vista Peak is a special place. We'd like to keep the charm and small-town feel."

Tasha considered his quandary. While she wasn't an architect, she had a similar love for historical structures. Zed's purple Victorian had ignited her love for old buildings.

"Have you thought of the idea of maybe marrying the past and present?" she asked.

"How so?"

"Maybe you could save a facade, or portion of the historic building, to honor the past, while integrating a newer, modern section."

A look of surprise exaggerated his features. His eyes lit up. "Tasha, you may be onto something."

She suppressed a smile, not wanting him to

know how much the idea that she'd helped him pleased her.

Neither of them broached the topic of the kiss before heading their separate ways. Though it had jettisoned her over the moon, it also confused her. Had he just been carried away by the romantic holiday? Had it really changed anything? She'd misread guys' signals before, jumping to conclusions and assuming what their actions meant, only to be let down and left heartbroken.

While he spent most of the day working on his project, she worked on her personal business plan and marketing ideas for the New Year. As she worked, she wrestled with the idea of when to tell Zed about her mother and his dad. She decided she'd make an amazing dinner, with candles and music, where she'd bring up the subject.

That evening, when she was done cooking, Tasha looked around the Victorian, admiring her handiwork. Candles flickered in the living room and dining room, creating a warm ambience. She'd put Milo in his favorite spot, sequestered in a cubbyhole in his bed in the finished attic. She hadn't wanted him to go on one of his erratic bends and leap on one of the tables, topple the candles and possibly burn the place down.

The sumptuous smell of pot lasagna, mingled with the sweet smell of apple pie bubbling in the oven, filled the house. She'd made Zed's favorites. Soft jazz poured from the sound system.

Tasha smoothed her cream sweaterdress, accented with chocolate-colored tights and toffee-colored boots. It was a favorite outfit of Zed's. A matching cameo choker necklace and shawl finished off the look.

She mentally rehearsed her confession to Zed about her mom and his dad. She figured she'd do it at the end of the meal, when he was satiated and happy.

She heard Zed's office door open and the creak of the stairs.

"Whew," she whispered. "Here we go."

Heading to the bottom of the steps, she waited for him to descend. "Hey," she said as he arrived on the landing.

Zed's eyes immediately roamed the candlelit house.

Was she imagining it, or did he seem subdued, different from the night before? Or was fear taunting her that her past would be her future and warning her not to open herself up to humiliation.

Because she felt awkward and didn't know what to do, she raised her hands dramatically. "Surprise!" she said. She heard the tremor in her voice.

Zed half smiled, but she saw his brow curl in curiosity.

"What's the occasion?"

"You. You're the occasion, Zed."

Something flickered in his light eyes, but just as quickly disappeared.

Tasha took his laptop bag and set it in the foyer. "Sit," she ordered. She pointed to the table. She'd decorated it with a lace tablecloth and fresh flowers.

Zed followed her orders, but after she brought out the second course with pot holders, he started to rise. "Can I help?"

"Nope."

He reluctantly sat back down.

When everything was on the table, she joined him. They said a prayer and ate. From the satisfied look on his face, Tasha knew Zed enjoyed the meal. However, as he finished each dish, her apprehension grew. Because when he was done, she was going to have to broach the subject she dreaded.

When Zed finished, he massaged his stomach. "That was amazing." He studied her. "Why do I feel like I'm being buttered up for something?"

"Would you like some coffee?"

"Not as much as I'd like to know what's really going on."

Tasha bit her lip. "Let's clear the table and go to the couch."

Zed obliged. They tag-teamed filling the dishwasher. After Zed helped her blow out the candles, they turned on the living room lamps and headed to the couch to sit.

Tasha gathered her courage.

"Is this about last night?" Zed said tentatively.

Tasha knew he was talking about the kiss. That amazing kiss that had left her breathless and feeling like she was floating on air. She shook her head. "I don't know where to begin."

Zed, apparently noticing her serious expression, straightened as if he was bracing himself for something.

"You know what I wish, Zed? I wish things could stay like they were yesterday. It was the most amazing day." She was embarrassed about the unexpected tears that sprung from her eyes.

Zed looked concerned. "Hey, it's okay."

She swiped her wet cheeks. "No, it's not, Zed. And I'm scared after I tell you what I'm about to, it will change everything."

"Give me some credit. I'm a big boy. I can take it."

Tasha gazed heavenward and gathered her resolve. "You know your aunt's letter that you gave me?"

He nodded.

"Well, it contained some pretty shocking news." Tasha considered how to best broach the subject. "For one thing, I learned our annual Christmas visits to your house might not have been as random as I thought."

Confusion darkened his features. "I don't get it."

Defeated, she slumped against the couch. "My mom knew your dad."

His eyebrows leaped in surprise.

She was suddenly so done with it all. She wanted to get it over with. "She didn't just know him. I think they had a relationship."

He froze. "I don't understand." She heard the coolness seep into his tone.

"I know it's unbelievable. I found out while talking to Vincent about my mom's past that your dad was the man my mom once loved. He said the man who broke up with her lived here. And your aunt's letter said your dad might have reignited a relationship with a childhood sweetheart."

Zed blinked several times, as if his brain was trying to clear out cobwebs and absorb what he'd heard.

"This is so hard for me," she said. "My mom and I were extremely close. I never thought in a million years she would have done something like this."

Zed's expression turned conflicted. "You're

telling me my dad and your mom had a relationship and you kept it from me?" He abruptly arose from the couch, rubbing his hands over his fade haircut.

"I'm so sorry, Zed."

"Tasha, you have to understand, I watched my mom's heart literally shrivel up and die. She suffered lifelong bouts of deep depression. And now you're telling me your mom might have contributed to her sorrow by stealing my dad's affection? This is difficult to hear."

She stood up, too. "Zed, please listen," she begged. "I didn't want any secrets between us. Last night was the best night of my life." Emotion constricted her throat. She swallowed hard, struggling to keep her composure. "You changed me. I wanted to open up to you. That's something I'd promised myself to never do again with a man, Zed. Ever."

Zed looked pained. "Tasha, if you're asking me to brush what your mother did under the rug, I'm not sure I can." His jaw tensed. "This is what I meant about relationships being impossible. They're messy." He looked pained. "Good thing ours has an end date."

She gasped. His words hit her like a sudden avalanche.

He walked past her and out of the room.

Chapter Thirteen

Tasha examined her face in the bathroom mirror. Her eyes were swollen and puffy from crying and lack of sleep.

The grief and sorrow of Zed's cool rejection was devastating. She had to admit to herself that in the back of her mind, she'd always thought that if the guys that rejected her had only stayed in the relationship long enough to really get to know her, they would have loved her. Zed's response provided a fatal blow to that theory.

Through the night she'd struggled with what to do. Milo, apparently sensing her mood, had jumped in the bed beside her.

She'd considered going back to her old studio. But beyond the anticipated payment, her integrity and the promise she'd made to Zed finally won out. She also remembered Zora's stipulation that a court-appointed spot check on their living arrangements might occur at any time. As hard as it would be, she decided to stay in the house with him until the agreement was up. The place was big enough that she could avoid him most of the time.

When she returned to her room after her shower, she found an urgent text from Pastor Landry, asking to see her immediately. A million scenarios ran through her head about why she was being summoned. Her intuition told her it couldn't be good.

She doctored her eyes the best she could, dressed, put on sunglasses and hoped it wouldn't appear too rude to wear them while talking with her pastor.

When she went downstairs to make a quick cup of coffee, she was grateful to find that it appeared Zed had already left for the day, evidenced by his dirty dishes neatly stacked in the sink and his missing satchel, which he always kept by the door.

She texted him about the meeting with the pastor and asked for his prayers. He texted back:

Want me to come along?

She texted:

No. But appreciate your prayers. Not sure what the meeting's about.

He texted back:

Praying.

Though she was grateful not to have to see Zed, it saddened her that he probably was purposefully avoiding her. It was the same pattern all over again. She opened her heart and made herself vulnerable and her heart was broken. When would she ever learn? How could she have been such a fool?

She drove to the church and mentally prepared herself as she walked up the path to the sanctuary. The bright Colorado day, with a gentle wind and majestic mountains bathed in light, belied what she knew she was about to face. Pastor Landry's terse text felt foreboding.

She walked into the lobby and down the long glass hallway to the administrative offices.

Sandy Kramer, the church secretary, was staring at her laptop screen, her fingers typing rapidly. The woman looked up at her and her fingers froze. Sandy's normal friendly expression was bland, like lukewarm water. "Good morning, Tasha." She might have been talking to a stranger, if Tasha didn't know any better. Sandy cocked her head toward the conference room. "They're waiting for you."

Tasha nodded. "Thank you." She started toward the wooden double doors to the conference room. A thought had her turning back to the secretary. "Sandy, thank you for always being so supportive of me."

A flicker of compassion flashed in her eyes. However, her expression remained dour.

When Tasha entered the conference room, Pastor Landry, Pastor Meltzer, a few deacons and several church board members were sitting around the conference room's oblong table. She guessed the empty seat at the end was for her. There might as well have been an interrogation spotlight cruelly beaming down over the chair. Her seat was separate from the cluster of other chairs.

"Tasha," Pastor Landry greeted her. "Please sit."

Tasha complied. She noticed the others in the room's eyes were glued on her.

"Would you like anything?" Pastor Landry asked. "We've got sparkling water, regular water, and I think there are some cookies leftover from the bake sale earlier this week." Although his offer sounded pleasant, Tasha heard tension in his voice.

She felt like a soldier at a firing squad being asked her order for the final meal. "No, thank you," she said.

Pastor Landry shuffled some papers in front

of him, then gathered them and drummed them against the table until they were one neat pile. "Tasha, first know that we love you," he said. His sea-blue eyes looked somewhere just past her, as if it was too hard to look at her directly.

She tried to say something, but her throat ached. She simply nodded her head in agreement with his words.

Pastor Eric Meltzer, the administrative pastor, sat up, bracing his shoulders. "As you know, Tasha, the Bible says that leaders are held to a higher standard. Pastor Landry shared with us your marriage arrangement."

Tasha's heart leaped in her chest.

"Pastor Landry wanted to get our take on the situation," Eric continued. "We are in agreement with him, that although this is a unique situation, the truth of it is that you are married. We feel you should give this relationship a chance."

Their words plunged into her heart like a knife and twisted. They were encouraging her to stay in the marriage. With a man who told her he would never commit himself to her or anyone else.

Her automatic defense mechanism response— to explain her desire to save Zed's family home, as well as her purpose to help sow into happy marriages by her new business plans, funded by money from the agreement—seemed moot. She sensed that this group had made up their minds about the matter.

Pastor Landry gave her a level stare. "Let's cut to the chase. We are putting you on a short hiatus as the singles' pastor and as the church's wedding planner. We'd like you to use this time to search your heart about your life. I realize we put undue pressure on you about marriage. I'm guessing this might have contributed to you feeling the need to do what you did, in entering into your unusual agreement." Although his tone didn't seem to ask a question, he studied her as if he was waiting for answer.

She nodded.

"That's what I thought. I implore you to use this time on hiatus to discover the source of your pain and ask for God's healing."

Tasha gulped. A sudden river of tears gushed from her eyes. "I've wanted to be married since I was seven. I saw what my mom went through as a single mom. Yet, like some *Groundhog Day* movie repeat, every guy I've ever cared for didn't want me. Do you know what that feels like—to think you would be such a blessing to someone, but to constantly be made to feel like you're no more than gum under their shoe? After the last breakup—by Christmas card, thank you very much—I was just done. I decided that I could love myself and give myself the best life. Because my dream had died."

Pastor Landry's neutral expression turned sympathetic. "Tasha, you need to understand something. We serve a God who can bring life, even from death. That's what we've celebrated these last three months—Jesus's birth at Christmas, our ultimate life-from-death hope, the New Year, symbolizing fresh opportunities, hopes and dreams, and Valentine's Day, the universal celebration of love and its possibilities. Maybe your issue wasn't only giving up on love but also giving up on the Author of Love, who's a master at writing new stories."

Tasha grabbed a tissue from her purse and dabbed her eyes.

Although inside she felt like wax melting in a fire, she bucked her shoulders back, held her head high, stood and walked out. As she passed Sandy, she noticed the woman's inquisitive gaze. Unable to speak, Tasha simply nodded and walked past the woman.

It was only when she was outside in her car that she fully caved in to the humiliation and regret she felt. Her phone pinged and she saw a text from Zed asking if she was okay. She gave him a simple "yes." Though she usually preferred phone calls over text, for once she was happy for the cut-and-dried ability of a text not to reveal the nuances and shades of emotion that a tone of voice could reveal during a conversation.

Zed texted back that he'd leave work immediately and meet her at home. Despite their recent coolness toward each other, she was touched that he wanted to be there for her.

When she arrived at the Victorian, Zed's car was already there. The smell of Chinese takeout greeted her nostrils as she entered the house.

Zed peeked from the kitchen. "I got dinner. Figured you might not be in the mood to cook."

"Thank you."

She took off her coat, hung it up and joined him in the kitchen. As they ate, she told him about the portion of the church meeting where they put her on hiatus to figure her life out. She left the rest of the conversation out.

"Know that I'm here for you," he said. "And maybe the hiatus is an opportunity to come back stronger and to be able to help the singles' group even more."

Right. For the terms and limits of our agreement, you're here. No more. No less.

"Some good mentor I've been."

Sympathy poured from his eyes. "Tash, don't beat yourself up. We're all works in progress. The best thing you can do is not try to be a symbol of perfection, which isn't possible anyway, but an example of imperfection—sometimes broken, but put back together by God. Besides, I think you underestimate how much they love you."

While his words comforted her, another thought wiggled into her consciousness. He believed her singles' group had a strong love for her, yet he himself did not. He was in the group with all the other men who had broken her heart and hadn't loved her enough.

Even though Pastor Landry talked about God's ability to bring life from death, God also gave people free will, and it was obvious nothing was going to happen with Zed. It was a good thing their time together was almost up. She was so done living in a fantasy world. It was time to swallow a deep dose of truth and move on.

Zed took one hand off the steering wheel and rubbed his temples. A mild headache threatened to blow up.

A car honked sharply, jolting him out of his reverie. He looked at the speedometer. He was going five miles below the speed limit. Man. That was a first. He was normally heavy footed on the gas pedal.

He sped up. Maybe subconsciously he was going slow because he dreaded the meeting that Anton had set up with him. His second sense told him Anton had something serious to talk to him about, but he knew he needed to just man up and get it over with.

Besides a few small disagreements that they'd quickly laughed off with an apology and a hug, they'd never had major differences. He truly considered Anton blood.

His best friend had agreed to meet him at Nate's Nest. Zed thought that would be easier than facing both Anton and Maya together at their home. Divide and conquer was his philosophy.

Finally arriving at the restaurant, Zed parked and exited the truck. "God, I need Your grace," he whispered. When he entered the restaurant, he instantly saw his best pal. Anton waved him over and gave him a bear hug.

"Hey," Zed said as he slipped in a booth seat.

"Hey." Anton's lips curved into a smile. "Thanks for agreeing to meet with me."

Zed nodded. His buddy stared at the menu like it had hidden secrets of the universe.

"I've missed you, man," Zed confessed.

"Same here, bud."

The waiter, a pimply-faced boy with a man bun, appeared. He had big St. Bernard kind eyes. "Wouldja like something to drink?"

"Coke, no ice. And I'm ready to order. I'd like a burger and fries."

The waiter scribbled the order on his notepad and disappeared.

He eyed Anton. "What are you thinking about ordering?"

Anton looked up. "Nothing, man. I'm just flirting with the menu. As much as I'm tempted to get something, Maya's got me on another one of her diets. Wifey's got me eating tofu, which I personally think tastes like boiled rubber bands, though that might be an insult to rubber bands."

Zed laughed.

Anton grabbed the salt shaker and tossed it from hand to hand. He finally sat the shaker down and gave Zed a level stare. "I say this because I love you, man. I think of you and what comes to mind is that the Lone Ranger rides again. The blustery cowboy with an iron heart that doesn't need anybody or anything. Here's the thing. I don't believe it's all fake with Tasha. You're different since her. Maya noticed it, too. While your arrangement started out a business thing, maybe it's serendipity that God put you together—two people who shunned the thought of love and commitment. Bro, you've got one of the biggest hearts of anyone Maya and I have ever known. I think God gave you that for a reason."

The waiter arrived with Zed's drink and refreshed Anton's. "Hey, man, I'm sorry. I forgot to ask how you wanted your burger."

"Well-done," Zed said.

"Good. Because they already started cooking it and it's way past the rare stage now."

Zed suppressed a chuckle.

When the waiter left, Zed turned his attention back to his friend.

"Some advice for you, bro," Anton began. "*The Lone Ranger* reruns were cool when we were kids. All stoic and full of bravado. A man's man. But really, it's sad. To never connect to anybody, to never receive love or give it. I think you need to ask yourself a question. Where do the lies and truth meet in your life?" Anton looked at his watch. "I better get going. Maya will be buggin' if I'm not home soon. She's got some couples yoga thing she wants us to attend together." Anton tentatively held out a hand for a fist bump. "So are we cool?"

"Yes, my friend." Zed nodded and returned his fist bump.

"You just called me *friend*. That's gotta be a good sign," Anton declared.

He dug a few dollar bills from his wallet and placed them on the table. "I think you've got a short window of time to do the work in here—" Anton pointed to his heart "—or it may be too late."

"Too late for what?" Zed asked.

"That's for you to figure out. Later, man." His friend turned and walked out of the restaurant.

Even though Anton's honesty stung, Zed was grateful for the friendship. He knew he could always trust Anton to be real and transparent and not play games. His relationship with Anton was all the more important when he considered his relationship with his dad. Zed took a gulp of his beverage, washing the cool, fizzy liquid around in his mouth before swallowing.

He and his father hadn't been on speaking terms before his sudden death of a heart attack.

All his life, his dad played a game of giving or taking his love, depending on Zed's actions. When he was younger, he'd desperately tried to please his father. He'd jumped through every hoop, met every demand—tried to be perfect. But because he was human, and by nature imperfect, he was doomed to failure. His father's way of loving was skewed, unhealthy and dysfunctional.

He'd called his father on the carpet about his actions, finally putting his foot down, refusing to give in to his father's cat and mouse game of love. And his father had cut off communications. The memory brought tears. Ashamed, he quickly wiped them away with his fist.

And people wondered why he thought relationships were messy, unwieldy. He bit his lip. Anton had criticized his lone-ranger mentality, and his points were valid, but Zed saw it from another perspective. Maybe the Lone Ranger was alone, but where Anton was wrong is that the Lone Ranger did have love. The one person he could depend on was himself. The one person he had control over loving was himself. And nobody could take that away.

That was where he saw the difference between himself and his mother. She'd let his father's actions and feelings toward her define her value and worth, and it had destroyed her.

Zed knew there was a reason the cowboy character had been a hero to him. The Lone Ranger hadn't waited for someone else to validate him. He was his own hero.

Chapter Fourteen

Conflicting feelings rolled through Zed as he drove to the Victorian. He'd made a decision about a few things after his talk with Anton. As much as he'd wanted his childhood home, to his shock, he realized it wouldn't be the same without Tasha. And letting her go was the best thing he could do for her to save her from him because he didn't know if he could give her all of his heart.

Though Tasha was still there with him in body because she was honorable about her commitment, it wasn't the same. The Victorian was just brick and mortar without the true meaning of home as a haven and a place of love, which the home had once symbolized.

He would tell his lawyer to sell the mansion to developers. The place mocked him. It seemed like an empty shell to him now. It was the end of an era, and it needed to be demolished.

Though he knew he'd made the right decision, his heart ached.

When he arrived at the Victorian, he parked out front and sat staring at the historic gem—a place that would soon be no more. It was a metaphor for his life. Time to move on. He texted his lawyer about selling before moving the truck into the garage. As he exited the garage, his neighbor, Mrs. Talmadge, waved at him.

"Afternoon, neighbor," she said cheerily.

"Hey, Mrs. Talmadge."

She was in her pajamas and pink robe. Her bottle-dyed platinum-blond hair was tied up in a matching pink scarf. Wispy curls peeked out from the edges. She had a mug of coffee in one hand and a newspaper was nestled under her other arm. "How are you and the new little missus doing?"

"Not so good, Mrs. Talmadge."

Compassion poured from her eyes. "Oh, dear. I'm so sorry."

"It happens," he said. He picked up his stride, hoping to communicate he was in a hurry, and gave Mrs. Talmadge a friendly wave. He felt her eyes on him as he neared the back door.

"I'm sure you don't need or want advice from an old lady," she said.

Zed guessed the elderly woman was ignoring

his silent body language cues that indicated he wished to be left alone.

"But I'm past the age of caring what people think," Mrs. Talmadge continued. "You young folks act surprised when lovey-dovey feelings disappear and when storms roll through. Like it was unexpected. But it's natural. Love is not a feeling. It's a commitment. One thing I know— that gal loves you. She looks at you like you are the sun, moon and stars."

Guilt gut-kicked him. Mrs. Talmadge's words confirmed his suspicions and the mistake he'd made cooking up such an impossible scheme to save the house. It hadn't been worth the emotional collateral damage.

Mrs. Talmadge smiled. "You look so much like your daddy. But the funny thing is, you're your mother through and through."

Her words stopped him in his tracks. Most people compared him to his father.

"I hit a nerve," she said.

He grimaced. "Don't get me wrong, Mrs. T. I loved my mother. But I hated how she gave my father the power to validate her worth. She always said she was nothing without him."

Mrs. Talmadge walked farther up her fence until she was closer to him. "Could that be why you keep your heart more secure than Fort Knox?"

Zed stopped and turned around. Mrs. Talmadge's expression was determined. Her chin jutted out. Her legs stood apart, as if she was prepared for a fight. "My family and I knew your Grandma Gigi. Even though I was just a little girl, I realized the woman was as close to perfect as they come, but she had her flaws."

Zed sighed. "Nobody's perfect," he said. *Least of all, me. Far from it.*

"I've never seen somebody with so much love in their heart. She had so much to give. And she gave it. She was like the real Pied Piper. She was always having less fortunate kids over at the house. She even temporarily put some of them up for a while, if they were having problems at home." Mrs. Talmadge chuckled. Then seriousness hardened her features again.

"But in giving all that love, all those pieces of her heart, nobody would have ever figured what would happen. Your dad lost out. She loved him the best she could, but it's like she belonged to the world. And she didn't have much left for him."

She paused and looked up at the bright blue sky. "I studied on it over the years. How could someone be so loving, yet their very family be deprived of their love? My husband, Hughes—God rest his soul—came up with the best answer. He said your grandmother loved your grandfather something fierce. When he died in that terrible accident, she was beyond devastated. And lost, I think. My husband said maybe mothering all the neighborhood kids was her way of trying to fill in for the great love she lost."

Zed gulped. He swallowed back tears for Gigi—and for his dad. He'd had no idea…

"Motherhood doesn't come with a training manual. We often learn as we go. We make mistakes. Your grandmother loved your father the best she could. But I think he felt cheated having to share her with others. I believe he made an unconscious vow to protect his heart, to never let himself be vulnerable enough for anyone to have that much power over him to hurt him.

"So he only gave part of himself. To your mother, and to you, too. He poured himself into his work to fill that hole inside him, just like Gigi did with mothering those kids." Mrs. Talmadge paused and momentarily stared past him, before continuing. "As a Black man, his fight for respect in his career was an uphill battle. I think when he finally found success, it made it sweeter. He thrived on that acceptance he got through his career, as a Black man who was finally accepted and valued."

If he was honest, Zed was like his father in this way, too. He prided himself in being one of the youngest deans at the university because of his expertise and acumen. Admittedly, he enjoyed the honor and acceptance that came with that.

"I think the respect your father got was a substitute for love he so badly craved for himself but couldn't give to others. But I also heard that part of his workaholic ways were so that you would have a better life and wouldn't have to suffer the impact of racism in the same way he did."

This declaration punched him in the gut. Had his dad's extreme focus on his career been his way of showing love and taking care of his family?

Mrs. Talmadge's blue eyes studied him for a moment, then her Yorkshire terrier, Misty, yelped and barked from the sliding glass door. Her withered hand reached out and patted Zed's arm. "You think you've won, because you've promised never to be like him, but have you, really?" Mrs. Talmadge observed him for a long moment.

Her words hit him in the gut. "My father wasn't exactly a role model. Did you and your family know about Violet-Sage?"

Mrs. Talmadge's eyes quickly widened and settled. "How did you find out about her?"

"Does it matter?" He heard the cold steel in his tone.

"Your father lived with the guilt of what happened."

Zed's patience was strained. "Some kind of

guilt. It wasn't enough to stop him from seeing her," he replied.

Mrs. Talmadge shook her head. "He felt he owed her that much. To help take care of her."

"No offense, Mrs. Talmadge, but I don't understand why you're defending him. I watched my mother's heart die on the vine."

Mrs. Talmadge stepped back from her fence. "You think Violet-Sage and your father were romantically involved?"

He stared at her, speechless.

"Violet-Sage was in love with your father's best friend, Chance Weathers. Chance and your dad were close as brothers. Chance even lived in the Victorian for a spell, when his parents were having some family problems. Your father convinced Chance to join the air force with him. When Chance was killed in a training mission, your dad blamed himself. He privately met with Violet-Sage as a friend. To assuage his guilt, I believe, he gave her money every now and then to help her out."

Zed attempted to absorb Mrs. Talmadge's news.

"As I mentioned earlier," she continued, "while you think you've won because you're not like your dad, have you really? In a way, aren't you just like him, by not fully opening your heart to anyone? How sad would it be to live in this world, and have all the world's riches, but not experience the true riches of life—riches of the heart?"

When he said nothing, she clucked her tongue. "Well, I've said my piece." With that, she turned and walked back to her house.

Zed suspected that she wished to leave him with his thoughts. His head hurt from all the thinking he'd been doing recently. But it couldn't begin to compare to how his heart hurt.

On his way into the house, he stopped to check the mail. He sifted through it as he walked. It was mostly advertisers' circulars. A letter sailed from the pile to the floor. He picked it up, noticing his lawyer's company emblem. After placing the other mail on a side table in the foyer, he ripped open the envelope from his lawyer.

His heart skipped a beat when he saw another letter inside the envelope, in his aunt Zora's handwriting. A yellow sticky was attached to it with a note from Michael, his lawyer.

Your aunt Zora requested this letter be given to you near the end of your three-month marriage agreement.

Zed had a feeling he needed to sit down to read the letter. He went into the living room and sank into an easy chair. He took a few deep breaths then unfolded the letter. His heart warmed at seeing her familiar handwriting.

My dearest nephew, I can imagine the shock on your face as you read this. Well, you know you shouldn't be surprised (smile). Your old aunt was always full of sugar and vinegar. I'm guessing you probably had conflicted feelings toward my odd will and the unusual arrangement I requested. You probably wonder why I would put our family home in jeopardy, not knowing what your ultimate response would be to my request.

Well, I felt it was worth the risk because I saw this big heart in you, even as a little boy—in the way you were often the little man of the house, how you fiercely loved your mother, and despite your father's selfishness, you loved him, too. Which was your choice. You could have hated him. But you were the bigger man. And I was counting on the belief that God didn't put all that amazing capacity to love in such a little boy without the desire for it to be shared.

I am optimistic that your love for the Victorian made you move forward to honor my request. I don't know how your three months turned out, but being a praying woman, who prayed for you all through the turmoil of your childhood, what I do know is how big our God is. And now that we, your family, are gone from the earth, your Heavenly

Father is watching over you and cheering you on for the most blessed life—if you will open your heart and receive the gift of love He offers you, however that shows up.

Because as much as you have a big heart to love others, God wants you to know love, too. I beg of you—break the family cycle. Don't let your parents' experience with love be your experience. I'm guessing you may think that you aren't worthy or don't deserve good things because of your past. Well, here's a little secret—none of us does. But God in His kindness blesses us not because of us, but because of Himself. And in case you didn't know, God did answer your prayer. Your mother did find love.

Shocked, Zed dropped the letter. He didn't know if his heart could take more secrets. He slowly picked up the correspondence and continued to read.

Your mother's last days she shared with me that she found out how much she'd been loved and valued by the Heavenly Father, who during all her hard times had been there, wanting to know her and show her who she really was—His precious, cherished, treasured daughter.

My dearest nephew, know that although your mother and I are no longer physically with you, our love will always be.

Forever and always.
Aunt Zora

Zed folded the letter and laid his head back on the easy chair. Memories from the past of moments in the house played on the movie screen of his mind, both the sad and good moments. He was beyond grateful to learn that his mother had found God's eternal love and she'd finally seen herself, through God's lens, as valued and loved.

He closed his eyes. "Lord, I want to forgive my parents for the ways they hurt me, I really do, just as You have forgiven me, as my Heavenly Father. Show me how." He didn't fight the tears that flowed. He felt, in a symbolic way, they were baptizing his past and washing it clean.

Tasha's life was like a ship lost at sea. Everything she'd thought her future held was now in shambles. She and Zed were cordial at home, but mostly still avoided each other.

The one thing stable in her life, ironically, was her blossoming relationship with her father. However, she needed to unpack their relationship history to move forward in a healthy way, so she was going to take him to dinner.

When she arrived at the assisted-living facility, her father was waiting in the circular drive in his wheelchair. A nurse's aide stood next to him. The woman helped her get her father into her car. His wheelchair was too big to fit in her tiny vehicle, so he'd brought his traveling cane. Although he could walk on his own, his balance was iffy sometimes.

She had to suppress a smile. He looked so cute. His wavy salt-and-pepper curls were neatly combed and slicked back, like a little boy taking his first elementary school photo. He wore a fresh, new, mint-colored shirt and crisply pressed jeans. One shirt pocket held a pocket protector with a pen and pencil and his glasses. He wore a leather jacket she'd gotten at a good deal from the thrift store.

After Tasha made sure he was securely in the vehicle with his seat belt on, she waved her thanks to the nurse's aide, who waved back before pushing the wheelchair back into the facility.

She let her father choose where he wanted to go, and he picked a classic all-you-can-eat chain restaurant. As she drove, he dipped his head out the window, like a happy dog gleefully enjoying the ride.

Although she liked seeing him happy, she

dreaded the difficult conversation she planned to have. When he'd found her, she'd experienced a host of emotions—shock, wonder, excitement, curiosity. But then had come the anger. She understood that her mom had blocked him from being in their lives after he chose college and his future over them. But he could have still fought to know her. Admittedly, her mother was formidable. But when you loved someone, you could practically move mountains. Yet, he hadn't moved a mountain to know her.

Upon their arrival at the restaurant, she helped him get seated. Tasha filled both their plates from the buffet line and returned to the table. Vincent was like a child with a new toy. His face glowed. It was obvious he didn't get out of the assisted-living facility much. They ate their food and made small talk.

When Vincent finished, pleasure blanketed his face. He eyed his remaining piece of lemon meringue pie. "I just want to admire it for a while," he said. He licked his lips. "Makes eating it much more enjoyable."

Tasha wiped her mouth with her napkin. "Vincent, I need to discuss something with you." She still hadn't been able to call him Dad or Father yet.

His eyebrows arched. "Yes, Love Nugget?"

Her heart pinged. "I don't know how to say

this." Heartburn bubbled in her throat. "I need to know why you didn't fight for me."

Surprise replaced his happy expression, and he fidgeted in his seat. He pushed the pie away. "Did you ply me with my favorite food to butter me up?"

"No," she said softly. "I simply wanted to bless you."

He smirked. "Why would you want to bless someone you don't trust?" Hurt flashed in his eyes.

"I didn't say I don't trust you. You must see this from my side. I didn't know about you, but you knew about me. I am your flesh and blood. Yet, you didn't fight to have a relationship with me. Was I not worth it?" Pain constricted her throat, so that her final words came out in an almost whisper.

Rather than looking at her, Vincent picked up his fork. He scooted the small amount of leftover food around on his plate. Then he ran the fork around the rim of the pie and poked the airy white meringue peaks. "Your mother was the love of my life. I'd loved her since we were six years old, when she first arrived in Miss McCutchen's class with her black rope of braids, bright lunch pail and shy smile."

Shocked, Tasha controlled her mouth from hanging open.

"Don't get me wrong," Vincent continued. "I loved my wife. But she wasn't my first choice. Bless her, she accepted second place. Just like I longed for Violet, your mother yearned for the love of her life—which wasn't me."

He sighed. "Broke my heart. When I offered to marry her after college, she made it clear she didn't want or need me in your lives. I guess my initial selfish choices cut too deep. To be honest, I was afraid every time I'd see you, I'd be reminded of her and what would never be mine. I was also afraid she'd probably turned you against me, too."

He shook his head several times. Crystal tears spilled down his brown-sugar-colored cheeks. "Tasha—the thought of being rejected all over again. I could not bear it." He wiped his eyes with the heels of his hands.

She swallowed the lump in her throat. "I thought you didn't want me."

"Oh, Love Nugget, not true. Not true. You were part of me. It would have been like cutting off my own arm to say I didn't want you. But my heart had been shattered once. I didn't know if I had the strength to survive it being broken again."

"If you were so afraid of that, what made you finally find me?"

He didn't answer right away, just nibbled on a

small piece of his pie. "I heard your mom died. I had some years and a life between our relationship and the past. I guess I felt stronger. When you get to a certain age, you get bolder, I think. You know you have less time. You know yourself better and what you want. You're often more willing to take a risk."

Tasha blew her nose and wiped her eyes. "I think I'm just now realizing something. All my life I've tried to get guys to love me—shamelessly begged them to, to the point of making a fool of myself. The wild thing is, it always backfired. I don't know. Maybe deep down inside I didn't feel I was worth loving, because the one man who should have wanted me didn't. The one man who should have wanted me abandoned me. Maybe I was trying to right the wrong of your rejection, but because I didn't love myself and feel worthy, I was drawing men to me that were all versions of you. Like a cruel vicious cycle."

Vincent observed her for a long moment before massaging his temples. "Tasha, we can't change the past. But what you can do is decide to change your future. Which you've started to do. Look at God's goodness. In the end, you got Zed. I can tell he's a good man."

She bit her lip so hard, she tasted blood. She dabbed her mouth with her napkin.

"Are you okay, honey?"

She stared into brown eyes that matched her own. She wanted to put on a front. But she simply couldn't. He'd been honest with her, and she needed to do the same. "No, I'm not. But I will be." She raised her chin high, in stubborn determination to fulfill her declaration.

"Trouble in paradise?"

She nodded. "The trouble is that I ever believed in paradise in the first place." Tasha admitted the truth about her and Zed's three-month arrangement and Zed's reluctance to marry due to his strained relationship with his dad and the choices his father had made.

After her confession, Vincent said nothing. But his brown hand reached across the table and clutched her fingers.

She had mixed feelings. Vincent's explanation had somewhat assuaged her emotions, but the hard ball of anger still rested, like an iron ball, in her gut. At the heart of it, her father had still rejected her. She was ashamed to admit that a part of her still wanted him to pay for it. It was an ugly part that she had to acknowledge.

God, help me.

God had chosen to forgive His rebellious children and made Himself vulnerable to them. Guilt rolled through her at the thought. God would require the same from her, as His child. Tasha thought of all the heartache she'd gone through with a long string of men that hurt her—crushed her spirit, even. If her father had fought for her and been in her life, would things have been different? Would she have had a healthier view of men because she'd been loved so well by her own father?

God, can we talk? To be honest, I'm not just mad at Vincent. I'm mad at You. I only say this because You already know it and You tell us to pour out our hearts to You. I see everybody around me blessed with love, except me. Like my client Shayla, who was barely in her twenties— almost half my age—when she found an amazing love and now is pregnant! Yet, I've waited almost double her lifetime, and the only thing I've gotten is a repeatedly broken heart and a sham marriage.

God, I'm weary. That's why I gave up hope of love. Because that way, I wouldn't be disappointed. And then You bring a man like Zed into my life. He's so amazing, but yet again, unattainable. Am I being disciplined? Do You have it in for me? Why, Lord?

She took even, deep breaths and let the warm tears flow as Vincent squeezed her hand.

Chapter Fifteen

Zed swiped the key fob to his university office and the door clicked open. He tossed his keys and laptop on the leather couch. Early-morning frost coated his office windows.

He collapsed on the couch. There was no way he could have stayed at the Victorian to clear his head and decide what he knew he must do.

Zed peered heavenward. "I'm sorry, Aunt Zora. I have to let the house go. Regardless of how much I love it." Zed cupped his head in his hands. While Gigi had made it a house filled with love, that was now the past. He'd failed Aunt Zora's test, and the place was more a facade— a shell of what it had been. Though he'd always thought his main reason for never marrying was to not be like his dad, a deeper fear curled the edges of his brain. Maybe he didn't have the capacity to love. Maybe he had a heart of stone.

He'd still pay Tasha for her time and would have done so even if not legally bound. It was time to let go of the past and accept his future.

His cell phone pinged. Vincent's number gleamed on the screen.

Zed answered. "Hey, Mr. Taliferro."

"Is this a bad time, son?"

"No—you're fine."

"I need to talk to you about Tasha. I've made bad decisions that affected her life. From what Tasha's told me, your dad made some similar choices. I'll make this short and sweet—please make me and your dad liars."

Surprised, Zed absorbed the man's words. "I'm sorry. I'm not tracking with you."

Vincent laughed. "I guess I'm being as clear as mud. What I mean is, your dad and I made decisions that made you and Tasha both think less of yourselves, that silently communicated that you weren't worthy of love. Make us liars by breaking the cycle, son. I'm not saying it will be easy and there won't be risks. That's just the nature of love."

Zed bit his lip. Emotions gurgled in his stomach. Anger shot through him from zero to sixty. There was a deep layer of unforgiveness still in his heart.

"I've laid a lot on you. I just ask you to think about it."

Zed tried to hold it together. "Thank you for calling, sir."

There was a pause on the other end of the line. His intuition told him Vincent was unhappy with his response and might be struggling to say more on the matter. Vincent finally sighed. "Goodbye, son."

Zed slammed his cell on the couch. Rapid-fire scenes of his childhood sped by in the movie screen of his mind—his mother's depression and bitter tears, the lonely nights after his dad would leave for his trips, and the constant ache in his heart at unfulfilled yearning for his father's attention.

A sudden image flashed through his mind of himself feverishly working, sometimes nonstop, trying to ignore the gnawing anger and pain that haunted him and using work as a balm.

Tasha's words came back to him, when she'd asked if he'd forgiven his father. "God, I don't know if I can forgive him—I feel like my heart is stone." Another revelation hit him: he also needed to forgive himself for not being able to make his mother happy, which spawned a fear he couldn't make anyone else happy, either.

Heated tears gushed from his eyes. He dropped to his knees. "God, I can't do this on my own. I need Your help!"

He grabbed his phone from the couch and tapped Anton's number.

"Hey, Zed." It was Maya. He inwardly groaned.

"Hi, Maya. Is Anton around?"

"He's at the gym. He forgot his cell."

"Oh. Okay."

"Zed, are you alright? You sound funny."

He wanted to hang up. His manly pride didn't want him weeping and being so broken in front of her. His best bud was who he needed.

"Zed, talk to me."

An involuntary sob escaped his lips uncensored.

"Zed! What's going on?"

Like pent-up water bursting from a dam, he spilled out everything about the call with Tasha's dad, along with his fears and the one thing he'd never admitted to anyone.

"Maya, I love Tasha."

There was a long pause on the other end. Then he heard sniffles.

"Now *you're* crying?" He wiped away tears, almost laughing at the absurdity of it all.

"Sorry. It's just that this is what I've been praying for."

"For me to be a wreck?" he cried.

She laughed and blew her nose. "No. From the first time you told us about the marriage agreement to save the house, I sensed there was more.

That maybe God was putting two hurt people together that had no other way to find each other unless they were forced to do so. And maybe this was His way of helping you both find love."

He half laughed and sobbed. "I'm a mess."

"Zed, God's in the cleanup business."

"I don't know if I can forgive my father."

"You can't," Maya said.

"What?"

"Jesus said that we can't do anything without our Heavenly Father. Ask for His strength and help to forgive your dad. Just remember how much He's forgiven you."

Zed took a deep breath and absorbed Maya's words. "Here's the other thing—what if I've blown it with Tasha? What if she won't give me another chance?"

"Zed, I'm guessing she loves you, too. I mean, how can she not?"

He gave a weak chuckle, before his doubt resurfaced. "I don't know about that. She's been hurt badly by men. And just when she thought I was different and she made herself vulnerable, I took a wrecking ball to her heart. Maya, if you saw the way she looked when I let her know things would definitely be over when the contract ended. She was devastated."

Maya sighed. "Here's my question to you, Zed."

She paused as if for added effect. "Is she worth taking the risk of your heart being broken?"

The next morning, as Tasha grabbed milk for her cereal, she looked at the calendar on the refrigerator door. Had it really been three weeks since Valentine's Day? The marriage agreement was just about up. And now she'd be able to go back to her life and try to rebuild it.

She couldn't deny deep grief and sorrow for what could have been. And for the spark of hope her relationship with Zed had reignited in her, causing her to ride a wave of euphoria and joy she'd never known. Until she crashed and burned. As much as she'd been hurt in the past, she'd finally thought she'd found real love—only to have her heart crushed yet again.

Just as she got cereal from the cabinet, her cell phone pinged. She looked at it.

It was a text from Zed, who'd left for work earlier.

Meet me at Union Station. Noon.

She attempted to quell her irritation. The terse message felt more like an order than an invitation. She guessed the reason he wanted to meet. Their three-month obligation was just about up. He probably wanted to discuss next steps. Since they'd started everything at Union Station, maybe he wanted to wind things up there, as well as meet her in a public place, just in case things went south. She knew the drill. When guys dumped her, all their earlier declarations of affection and civility dissolved.

Even so, it still hurt that he could treat her like nothing more than a business transaction. A means to an end. But that was what she'd agreed to. Now he had what he wanted, his beloved home. She couldn't totally fault him since she'd also have money for her business.

Tasha waited for the normal feelings of rejection to overtake her. Instead, her chest rose with a new sense of resolve. *I'm a good person—a great person. I deserve to be loved and I would be a wonderful gift to somebody. Even if treasure is never discovered, that doesn't mean it's not treasure and valuable.*

She decided to girl up and just deal. She owed herself that, and she was done with letting any man define her value. God loved her and said she was special. That was all she needed to know. Even if nobody else loved her, she could and would love herself.

She texted Zed back, confirming she'd be there, then changed out of her dowdy beige T-shirt and faded jeans. After putting on a fuchsia sweater, pink-and-navy-blue plaid pants and navy blue loafers, she tied her sandy-brown curls back with a pink ribbon and added diamond post earrings that had belonged to her mother. Before she walked out the door, she threw on her favorite short aqua winter coat and her pink sunglasses.

When she arrived at Union Station, she immediately spotted Zed sitting on one of the vintage benches. He rose when she approached.

"Hey," he said.

"Hey."

"How are you doing?" His eyes searched hers.

"Oh, I'm just peachy keen," she said, repeating a phrase her mother had often used. "The world is my oyster," she replied. "Not."

"We need to talk," Zed said.

"I thought that was what we were doing." She'd meant to be funny, but heard the edge in her tone.

He gave her an odd look and then took her hand. "Follow me."

He led her to Snooze, where there was an empty table waiting for them.

"How did you get a table so fast?"

"I made reservations."

"Go you," she quipped.

When they sat, he immediately took an envelope from his crisp black jacket. He laid it between them but kept his hand on it. "First, I want to thank you for your assistance."

My assistance? Something about his words stung. Even though she knew their arrangement had been nothing more than a business deal, it hurt that he could be so matter-of-fact about it all.

"I guess we both got what we wanted," she said.

"Yes and no," he said.

"What does that mean?" She wasn't in the mood for verbal gymnastics or riddles. She'd had enough unanswered questions in her life. Now she just wanted the truth. Plain and clear.

His heart pounded like a jackhammer. The look of defiance and hurt on Tasha's face nearly slayed him. Was she beyond the point of no return, in terms of their relationship? Had he made a mistake meeting her here? Was he about to be humiliated? Maya's question about whether Tasha was worth the risk, which sounded noble and courageous at the time, now didn't pack as powerful a punch. He decided to push ahead, all the while quaking in his boots.

"First, you were wrong about your mother and my dad," he said.

He wanted to take her hand, but decided against it, afraid she would recoil. "Your mom didn't have a relationship with my dad." He told her what Mrs. Talmadge had revealed to him.

He could tell she was trying to contain herself. "That's good to know," she replied, her voice shaky. "I had a hard time believing she could have been a home-wrecker. It makes me sad about her lost love, though."

"I partially blamed your mother for my family's miserable life. Turns out, maybe I'm to blame, too," Zed said.

"How do you mean?"

"I think I used the suspicion about your mother and my dad as an excuse because I was afraid. Afraid to fully give my heart to anyone. I blamed my aversion to marriage on my dad. And that was part of it. But I was my mother's son and I adored her. I think I silently vowed to never be vulnerable enough to let someone ever hurt me the way she was hurt by my dad. My past, with my parents' mistakes, was like a one-two punch. Funny thing is, I was trying so hard to not be like my father that I became just like him. I put my heart on permanent lockdown."

"The lockdown part I got," Tasha replied.

"You didn't let me finish. I was on lockdown—until you, Tash."

"Me?" she said.

"Your dad called me the other day. He challenged me to make him and my father liars by fighting for you, like they never did when we were kids. Tasha, love was something I never could admit I wanted. I never thought I deserved it. Because that's what my dad's actions silently told me and my mom. And I believed it. But here's what I learned—the past happened. It hur⬤ I can't change it, or the decisions others made. But I can change how I respond to it and how it affects my future. That's the blessing God gives. He can restore us and set us free from the past."

He quietly observed her. "Tash, I don't like messy, I don't like things being out of control and I don't like the unknown. But you made me not care about those things as much as I care about you. And I've realized when God is the God of our lives, that means He brings His power to our messes, and is God of them, too, if we'll let Him."

"Look," Tasha said, "I've been down this road before with noncommittal guys who said they 'cared' for me." She made air quote signs with her fingers. "Caring about somebody isn't the same as love. You once told me that you wouldn't give yourself to anything unless you could give all of you. If I've learned anything in these past three months, it's that I shouldn't settle for less. I deserve the best."

He sighed as sadness engulfed him. "I can't promise you that."

Tasha bit her lip. Her expression looked as if his words had shredded her heart, like glass shards, piece by piece.

"Tash," he said softly.

She avoided his gaze. Instead, she watched a

ivacious couple walking by their table, laughing profusely.

"I can't promise you that because I'm not the best me right now. I'm a work in progress. Kinda like Prince Charming with a cracked crown." His hand caressed her cheek. Then his forefinger turned her face toward his.

"Here's what I can promise you. I'll be a husband who trusts the Lord to heal my broken places and restore me. I'll trust God and open my heart to Him to do what He needs to make that happen so I can be the best husband, the best man, for you that I can. All I can promise you is that I love you."

She hiccuped and swallowed hard. "Stop it! Just stop it now!"

He recoiled. Had he just put his heart on the chopping block? Had his love been thrown back in his face, the one time he opened his heart?

"Now, see, that look—that look right there, do you have any idea how devastating that is?" she cried.

He shook his head in confusion. "What are you talking about?"

"That look, emanating from your eyes right now—it can melt steel, planets, maybe even galaxies! It's how I always wanted a guy to look at me. It's not fair you should have such superhuman powers."

He chuckled, relief washing over him.

Fresh tears bathed her face. She quickly wiped her cheeks. "You really love me?"

"Why do you find that so hard to believe?"

"Because whenever I've been in love with someone, it was never reciprocated. And the funny thing is, I realize now that what I thought was love with the men in my past was paltry and shallow compared to what I feel for you. I am so very in love with you, too, Zed Evans. Cracked crown and all."

Her gaze dropped to the envelope he was holding, and her eyes narrowed. "Hey, is this your way out of having to pay me for my services?" The humor in her voice relieved him.

He didn't censor a hardy chuckle. He pushed the envelope he'd been holding her way. She opened it and found a check for the amount he'd promised.

His phone pinged. He slipped it out of his jacket pocket and read the message on the screen, his eyes widening.

"Zed, what is it?"

He was amazed. "I contacted my lawyer to start proceedings to sell the Victorian to developers."

"What!" Tasha cried. "How could you even consider such a thing?"

"I know. I surprised myself, too. But without

you, the place had no meaning for me. I realized I'd always have memories of my mother. Nobody can take those from me. Anyway, I hadn't heard from my lawyer. He just texted that he's been out of town because of a family emergency and just saw my message. The house isn't sold!"

"Oh, Zed!" Tasha clasped her hands and looked heavenward, probably giving a silent thank-you to God.

"Let me text him that our plans have changed and to cancel everything. You and I can live in the Victorian and I can rent out my home. You know, I think that's what Aunt Zora hoped for all along—that love would make the house a home again. I believe love was the legacy she wanted to live on." Zed's thumbs quickly moved across his phone keyboard. When he was done he slowly dropped to one knee.

Several restaurant patrons looked their way.

"What are you doing, Zed?"

"Asking you to marry me."

"But we're already married, goofball," she declared.

"But in spirit as well as in body this time. And forever," he answered.

"Oh, Zed! Yes! Yes!" she yelled excitedly. "You'll never get rid of me!" She took out her phone. "Can you hold on for a moment?"

"Really?" he said.

"Seriously," she pleaded. "It'll just take a sec."

Curious, he leaned over and read the screen as she typed. She was texting Kelly.

I took your advice. I got back up again—and you were right. He loves me to the moon and beyond! More later!

Within seconds heart emojis and exclamation points rolled across her screen. She laughed, before returning her attention to Zed.

"Zed Evans, I'll be the peanut to your butter, the stick to your glue, the color to your crayon—"

He swiftly rose and kissed her, interrupting her silly declarations.

"I see you still got jokes," he said tenderly, after the kiss.

"More important, I've got you," she replied. Her eyes sparkled.

His heart danced.

"Let's go home, my missus."

"Yes, my mister."

* * * * *

If you enjoyed this book, pick up these other sweet romances from Love Inspired.

An Amish Baby for Christmas
by Vannetta Chapman
The Amish Outcast's Holiday Return
by Lacy Williams
The Prodigal's Holiday Hope
by Jill Kemerer
The Path Not Taken
by Ruth Logan Herne
Snowed in for Christmas
by Gabrielle Meyer

*Find more great reads at
www.LoveInspired.com*

Dear Reader,

I hope you enjoyed spending time in Zed and Tasha's world. I loved writing the story of these two broken people who were stuck in emotional prisons that prevented them from being able to love and be fully loved. That is, until their forced proximity offered God a chance to put a mirror up to their lives and to show His power and ability to bring life from dead situations.

I also loved the idea of reversing their bad holiday experiences of the past. Additionally, I enjoyed weaving the Victorian's history, which was like a third character, into their story. Finally, Union Station in Denver is one of my favorite buildings. I purposely started their healing journey there and ended it there with their "union." Thank you for entrusting me with your precious time, as you experienced Tasha and Zed's story.

C.J. Carroll

Get 4 FREE REWARDS!

We'll send you 2 FREE Books plus 2 FREE Mystery Gifts.

Love Inspired books feature uplifting stories where faith helps guide you through life's challenges and discover the promise of a new beginning.

FREE Value Over **$20**

YES! Please send me 2 FREE Love Inspired Romance novels and my 2 FREE mystery gifts (gifts are worth about $10 retail). After receiving them, if I don't wish to receive any more books, I can return the shipping statement marked "cancel." If I don't cancel, I will receive 6 brand-new novels every month and be billed just $5.24 each for the regular-print edition or $5.99 each for the larger-print edition in the U.S., or $5.74 each for the regular-print edition or $6.24 each for the larger-print edition in Canada. That's a savings of at least 13% off the cover price. It's quite a bargain! Shipping and handling is just 50¢ per book in the U.S. and $1.25 per book in Canada.* I understand that accepting the 2 free books and gifts places me under no obligation to buy anything. I can always return a shipment and cancel at any time. The free books and gifts are mine to keep no matter what I decide.

Choose one: ☐ **Love Inspired Romance Regular-Print** (105/305 IDN GNWC) ☐ **Love Inspired Romance Larger-Print** (122/322 IDN GNWC)

Name (please print)

Address _____ Apt. #

City _____ State/Province _____ Zip/Postal Code

Email: Please check this box ☐ if you would like to receive newsletters and promotional emails from Harlequin Enterprises ULC and its affiliates. You can unsubscribe anytime.

Mail to the Harlequin Reader Service:
IN U.S.A.: P.O. Box 1341, Buffalo, NY 14240-8531
IN CANADA: P.O. Box 603, Fort Erie, Ontario L2A 5X3

Want to try 2 free books from another series? Call 1-800-873-8635 or visit www.ReaderService.com.

---

*Terms and prices subject to change without notice. Prices do not include sales taxes, which will be charged (if applicable) based on your state or country of residence. Canadian residents will be charged applicable taxes. Offer not valid in Quebec. This offer is limited to one order per household. Books received may not be as shown. Not valid for current subscribers to Love Inspired Romance books. All orders subject to approval. Credit or debit balances in a customer's account(s) may be offset by any other outstanding balance owed by or to the customer. Please allow 4 to 6 weeks for delivery. Offer available while quantities last.

Your Privacy—Your information is being collected by Harlequin Enterprises ULC, operating as Harlequin Reader Service. For a complete summary of the information we collect, how we use this information and to whom it is disclosed, please visit our privacy notice located at corporate.harlequin.com/privacy-notice. From time to time we may also exchange your personal information with reputable third parties. If you wish to opt out of this sharing of your personal information, please visit readerservice.com/consumerschoice or call 1-800-873-8635. **Notice to California Residents**—Under California law, you have specific rights to control and access your data. For more information on these rights and how to exercise them, visit corporate.harlequin.com/california-privacy.

LIR21R2

Get 4 FREE REWARDS!

We'll send you 2 FREE Books
<u>plus</u> 2 FREE Mystery Gifts.

Harlequin Heartwarming Larger-Print books will connect you to uplifting stories where the bonds of friendship, family and community unite.

FREE
Value Over
$20

YES! Please send me 2 FREE Harlequin Heartwarming Larger-Print novels and my 2 FREE mystery gifts (gifts worth about $10 retail). After receiving them, if I don't wish to receive any more books, I can return the shipping statement marked "cancel." If I don't cancel, I will receive 4 brand-new larger-print novels every month and be billed just $5.74 per book in the U.S. or $6.24 per book in Canada. That's a savings of at least 21% off the cover price. It's quite a bargain! Shipping and handling is just 50¢ per book in the U.S. and $1.25 per book in Canada.* I understand that accepting the 2 free books and gifts places me under no obligation to buy anything. I can always return a shipment and cancel at any time. The free books and gifts are mine to keep no matter what I decide.

161/361 HDN GNPZ

Name (please print)

Address   Apt. #

City   State/Province   Zip/Postal Code

Email: Please check this box ☐ if you would like to receive newsletters and promotional emails from Harlequin Enterprises ULC and its affiliates. You can unsubscribe anytime.

Mail to the **Harlequin Reader Service:**
IN U.S.A.: P.O. Box 1341, Buffalo, NY 14240-8531
IN CANADA: P.O. Box 603, Fort Erie, Ontario L2A 5X3

Want to try 2 free books from another series? Call 1-800-873-8635 or visit www.ReaderService.com.

*Terms and prices subject to change without notice. Prices do not include sales taxes, which will be charged (if applicable) based on your state or country of residence. Canadian residents will be charged applicable taxes. Offer not valid in Quebec. This offer is limited to one order per household. Books received may not be as shown. Not valid for current subscribers to Harlequin Heartwarming Larger-Print books. All orders subject to approval. Credit or debit balances in a customer's account(s) may be offset by any other outstanding balance owed by or to the customer. Please allow 4 to 6 weeks for delivery. Offer available while quantities last.

Your Privacy—Your information is being collected by Harlequin Enterprises ULC, operating as Harlequin Reader Service. For a complete summary of the information we collect, how we use this information and to whom it is disclosed, please visit our privacy notice located at corporate.harlequin.com/privacy-notice. From time to time we may also exchange your personal information with reputable third parties. If you wish to opt out of this sharing of your personal information, please visit readerservice.com/consumerschoice or call 1-800-873-8635. **Notice to California Residents**—Under California law, you have specific rights to control and access your data. For more information on these rights and how to exercise them, visit corporate.harlequin.com/california-privacy.

HW21R2

HARLEQUIN SELECTS COLLECTION

19 FREE BOOKS IN ALL!

From Robyn Carr to RaeAnne Thayne to Linda Lael Miller and Sherryl Woods we promise (actually, GUARANTEE!) each author in the Harlequin Selects collection has seen their name on the *New York Times* or *USA TODAY* bestseller lists!